DOWN AGAIN TO THE DEEP

DOWN AGAIN TO THE DEEP

Joan Calmady-Hamlyn

The Book Guild Ltd
Sussex, England

This book is a work of fiction. The characters and situations in this story are imaginary. No resemblance is intended between these characters and any real persons, either living or dead.

This book is sold subject to the condition that it shall not, by way of trade or otherwise, be lent, re-sold, hired out, photocopied or held in any retrieval system or otherwise circulated without the publisher's prior consent in any form of binding or cover other than that in which this is published and without a similar condition including this condition being imposed on the subsequent purchaser.

The Book Guild Ltd.
25 High Street,
Lewes, Sussex

First published 2000
© Joan Calmady-Hamlyn 2000

Set in Times
Typesetting by IML Typographers, Chester, Cheshire
Printed in Great Britain by
Bookcraft (Bath) Ltd, Avon

A catalogue record for this book is
available from the British Library

ISBN 1 85776 479 X

1

The office was dark and shabby, the walls institutional custard cream and the woodwork painted brown. The top of the window was open a few inches and from outside came faint sounds to break into the silence of the room: the sound of marching feet, the sound of a distant voice, the sound of a ship's siren far out on the river.

Captain (D), the O.C. of the destroyer flotilla, seated at the desk heard the sounds without noticing them. They were customary ones that made up his day. Before him was a sheaf of closely typed foolscap pages. An adjustable calendar to the rear of his desk proclaimed the date to be 30 June 1938.

The door opened to admit a seaman messenger.

'Lieutenant-Commander Sillifant, sir,' he said and stood aside to let a tall dark-haired officer, cap tucked under his arm, come into the office.

'Hullo, Peter, come in and sit down,' said Captain (D).

'Thank you, sir.'

Peter Sillifant was 30 years old and had served in the Royal Navy for 17 years. He was a native of Devon and this, apparently, had some bearing on the fact that he had been sent for from his destroyer at present on the trot in the river.

'You come from these parts, don't you, Peter?' said Captain (D). 'Do you know Seahaven?'

'Quite well, sir. Nice little port, well-found dockyard, pleasant town.'

'It seems they're celebrating their centenary since they got their charter or whatever. Must say they sound like a seaside bungalow or something. Anyway, they would like a naval presence for a few days – you know the form – cocktail party at the Dockyard

Manager's, Mayoral lunch, visits to the ship by the town notables, so on. I'm sending you.'

'Yes, sir. Why me?'

'Two reasons. You know the place for one.' Captain (D) flipped the pages on his desk. 'Seen the half-yearly promotion list, yet?'

'Er – yes, sir.'

The Captain grinned.

'I didn't congratulate you first, Commander,' he said. 'Thought I might spring it on you! Anyway, that's the second reason and I'd like you to get your third stripe up, now. Seahaven, it appears, is brass rags with Seehaven in north-east Germany who are sending a ship, also called *Seehaven*. She's commanded by a three-ringer – *Fregatten-Kapitän* I think they call it – and I want an equal C.O. there.'

'Do we know anything about him, sir?'

'A bright spark, I believe. Name's Dettner. He came over in the *Graf Spee* to the Coronation Review last year so I expect he speaks English.'

'Helpful, of course,' said Sillifant, with a grin. 'My German's not too hot.'

Captain (D) stirred restlessly.

'Why did they have to have a centenary this year?' he moaned. 'You know how dicey the situation is, Peter. I don't want a political incident.'

'No, sir. When do they arrive?'

'Due to berth at eleven hundred hours on Thursday. You'd better be there at ten. Tuesday today – that'll give you time to put your stripes up. Better sail at zero-eight-thirty to be sure. Here are the cards – drinks party, Thursday evening, Mayoral lunch, Friday, cricket match on Saturday afternoon – no, you don't have to supply a team – followed by the Marines' band Beating Retreat in the evening and church parade at St Ordulph's Sunday morning. Then you're free to go.'

'Town leave, sir?'

'Ye-es. At your discretion.'

Peter chuckled.

'I cannot imagine *Fregatten-Kapitän* Dettner being madly excited at the cricket match, can you, sir?'

'You never know. He might be a sports fanatic.'

'Strength through joy? I thought that was cruising – or wandering in the woods.'

'Don't make difficulties, Peter. If you want any advice on how to behave come and see me. Otherwise, I wish you luck and Godspeed.'

'Thank you, sir.'

The new Commander Peter Sillifant stood up and departed from the shabby office and from the base. His steward had already taken his other uniforms to the tailors for the adjustment of his rank badges and he stopped off there to swap his jacket and to purchase his new gold-leafed cap. Somewhat self-consciously he proceeded to the quayside and awaited his boat transport to the destroyer swinging at her buoy.

The ship's First Lieutenant, Jasper Hare, awaited him at the top of the accommodation ladder. A rather gangling man with crisp, short, brownish hair and a benevolent face, totally unlike anyone's idea of a Jasper, it was inevitable that Number One should be called Bunny. He and Peter had known each other since Dartmouth days although this was their first commission together.

'We're going to a party, all on our own!' Peter told him and led him below to fill in the details.

So with the destroyer, HMS *Curre*, snugly berthed at No. 8 wharf in Seahaven's inner basin, Commander Peter Sillifant and Lieutenant Bunny Hare made their last checks to ensure that everything was in order, the Union flag at the jackstaff, the White Ensign at the stern, both hanging limply in the early July morning heat.

They had regained the bridge when a signalman, standing just below them on the superstructure, sang out ' 'Ere she comes, sir,' and put his binoculars back up to his eyes.

'Where's she berthing, Number One?' asked Peter.

'No. 7 wharf, sir – just ahead of us.'

They watched the approaching destroyer keenly, admitting to themselves that they were looking for faults or for an error in navigation. The vessel had the red, black and white Nazi ensign flying from the peak and came steadily into the basin until her raking stem was just short of *Curre*. Then, with a flurry of white water at her stern she came to a halt, about half a ship's length out from the quayside. Then, gently and with great dignity, she executed a perfect 16-point turn and slid quietly into her berth. The ensign came down from the peak and simultaneously another was broken out at the stern.

'It's absolutely spot-on eleven hundred hours,' murmured Bunny, awestruck.

He and Peter looked at each other.

'I think *Fregatten-Kapitän* Dettner is someone to be reckoned with,' said Peter, grimly.

' 'E's signalling, sir,' called the Bunts, below them. '"C.O. to C.O. May I pay you an informal visit?"'

'We're being out-manoeuvred, Bunny,' said Peter. 'Make back "Delighted. Come aboard."'

As the lamp clacked his reply he turned to go below. 'Informal or not, better get a side party. Meet him, will you, Number One and bring him to the wardroom.' He paused and looked back. The German captain was already descending the brow from his quarterdeck. 'Smack it about – he'll be there before you are!'

Bunny disappeared abruptly and hurried aft, collecting a couple of seamen on the way to reinforce the Quartermaster and the Officer of the Watch on the quarterdeck.

Dettner was a slenderly-built man, a little above medium height. His uniform was immaculate and of excellent cloth, Bunny noted. As he came up the brow and stepped on to the deck he saluted – a naval salute, thank God, thought Bunny, not the Nazi one. He had a thin, browned face and keen, blue eyes which swept over the scene and made the side party stiffen spontaneously.

'Welcome aboard, sir,' said Bunny. 'Will you come below?'

He led the way down to the wardroom and Dettner took off his cap and tucked it under his arm, revealing short, blond hair.

Peter came forward to greet him, holding out his hand.

'This is very civil of you,' he said.

'Did you mind?' The man smiled, disarmingly. 'I've not done this before and I had no idea if I should put on my sword and make an official visit. I thought perhaps you could guide me through this programme.'

Peter laughed outright. The opening was so totally different from what he had been expecting. He did not entirely believe what the man said, however. He was pretty sure that the form of such port visits and the protocol to be observed was well-known to the *Fregatten-Kapitän*.

'Sit down, Captain,' he said. 'Number One, rustle up some coffee, please.'

Bunny had already seen the leading steward hovering and signed to him.

'We were admiring your entry into the basin, sir,' he remarked.

'What one would call a turn on the centre, I believe,' said Peter.

The blue eyes contemplated them as though the man sought to get the measure of the British officers and the slightly teasing note in Peter's voice.

'If one were a horseman, I believe that is so,' he said. 'I saw you watching – so I was showing off. Thank God, it succeeded.'

Peter did not entirely believe that, either. However, coffee served, he pulled out the sheet detailing the four days' programme from his pocket.

'What can I tell you, Captain?' he asked.

'Drinks, this evening. Mess kit? And who is likely to be there?'

'Not mess kit. The Dockyard Manager and his senior staff will be there – with wives, I expect. Mayoral lunch, all the civic dignitaries, the Chief Constable, Lord Lieutenant, so on.'

'Chief Constable?'

'Head of Police,' said Peter.

'Not like your Gestapo Chief,' said Bunny and could have bitten his tongue out.

For an instant Peter had a vision of the cartoon showing a chamber pot with the caption 'Jest-a-po'. Somehow he did not think the *Fregatten-Kapitän* would be amused.

'Cricket match on Saturday. You could, I think, send a substitute to that. But will you and your Number One come on board for Beating the Retreat and dine with us, afterwards?' He glanced at Bunny for approval.

'Yes. Thank you. And the Church Parade?'

'I think they are reserving places for five officers and twenty men, from each ship.'

'Good. Will you be sailing immediately or will you and Lieutenant Hare have lunch with us?'

'Thank you.' Peter glanced at Bunny again. 'We'd be pleased to.'

Dettner looked at his watch and stood up.

'Thank you for your help. We shall meet this evening. I must go now and get my sword. I have an appointment with the German Consul at noon.'

Number One escorted him to the brow and watched his rather quick-striding walk back to his own ship. Then he went back to the wardroom and he and Peter exchanged a long look.

'Captain (D) said he was a bright spark,' said Peter. 'I think I would say a live wire.'

2

Fregatten-Kapitän Dettner continued to show his one-upmanship, to Peter's chagrin, when the Dockyard Heads of Department had a two-hour tour of the German ship that afternoon. Consequently he and the two officers accompanying him at the cocktail party that evening were acquainted with their hosts while Peter, Bunny and the Pilot who made up their party, had yet to meet them.

The following day, the Mayoral car collected both C.O.s from the docks and sped them through the town square and out to the Guildhall. As they passed through the Square, Dettner surveyed it rather anxiously.

'What's the matter?' asked Peter.

'I have given my men four hours' shore leave,' said Dettner. 'And there are too many public houses in the Square.'

'So've I,' said Peter. 'Let's hope they don't clash.'

The Mayor, the Lord Lieutenant, the Chief Constable, the Town Clerk and sundry minions were already gathered in the Guildhall, the Mayor looking somewhat overheated in his robes as did the Lord Lieutenant and the Chief Constable in their uniforms. Their respective wives in summer dresses looked much more comfortable. After a flurry of handshakes and bows from the German captain, who put the wives' hands to his lips with great correctness, the uniformed quartet were able to shed caps, gloves and swords and indulge in a glass of sherry prior to lunch.

The speeches were, fortunately, not too lengthy. The Mayor spoke of the granting of the port charter in 1838, the Lord Lieutenant enlarged on the same theme, the Chief Constable lauded the relative lack of crime and Dettner, as concise as ever, conveyed greetings from the port of Seehaven and expressed the wish that the concord between the two ports would continue.

Afterwards, as they drank coffee in the Mayor's Parlour, he remarked to Peter that fulfilment of that wish seemed to be unlikely.

'You expect war?' said Peter.

'I would like to think I would be making a third visit to England next year but I do not have great hopes.' The blue eyes swept the assembled guests. 'Now that the Lord Lieutenant has gone and the Chief Constable is going, can we count ourselves next in seniority?'

The Chief Constable was approaching them to say goodbye and when he had left, Peter agreed. They made their farewells to the Mayor and his Mayoress and went out to collect their accoutrements. The crested car drew up at the steps as they descended.

It seemed that Dettner's foreboding was right. The Chief Constable's car had stopped at the top of the road leading into the Square and he was out and surveying the fighting groups of British and German sailors. The Mayor's chauffeur pulled up alongside.

Dettner did not wait. He stripped off his sword and belt and got out of the car. His voice, calling the *Seehaven* men to attention, reached across the Square as, Peter felt, it had probably reached to the masthead in his sail training days. The men, hesitant at first, came to some sort of order and Peter was thankful to see that none of the *Curre*'s men took advantage of them. He went forward to the Chief Constable whose forces were gathering.

'Could we keep the police out of this, please, sir?' he said and watched Dettner single out a leading rate and order him to form up the men and march them off. Seeing one of his own leading hands, Peter signed to him to follow suit.

'Well, thank God for that,' said the Chief Constable and they watched the slight figure come back across the Square. From the look of anger in his eyes, Peter did not envy the libertymen when he got back on board. He, himself, he realised, would have to conduct an enquiry into the cause of the fight.

Dettner reached them and saluted the Chief Constable.

'I must apologise,' he said. 'There will be no more shore leave.'

'Thank you, Captain Dettner,' said the Chief Constable. 'I will leave the matter in your hands. And yours also, Commander.

'Yes, sir. I must apologise, too, for my men's behaviour.'

'Well, well.' The Chief Constable smiled, bleakly. 'Seamen ashore and plenty of pubs. It's been happening since before Nelson's time.'

In the car again, Peter said 'My Number One's organising some swimming and sailing sports this afternoon. Would your men join in?'

'Thank you, yes. I am sure they would be pleased. I will get my First Lieutenant to liaise, h'n?'

'Yes. Neutral ground! Dockside, here, in half an hour.'

The car drew up midway between the two ships and the C.Os. got out. Dettner turned to thank the chauffeur and from what Peter could see, tipped him quite liberally. They both paused for a while to look at the peaceful scene, under the blue sky and the bright afternoon sun.

'It is near to Dartmoor here?' asked Dettner. 'I thought if it is possible – and I do not have to watch the cricket match – I would like to visit there.'

'How much time would you have to spare?'

'Say from ten hundred hours until it is time to prepare for your Marines.'

'Buses and trains could be a bit awkward.' Peter considered. He went on slowly, 'I live on Dartmoor. May I show it to you?'

He was not sure what had prompted him to make the offer unless it was a desire to show this tautly-strung man the wildness and majesty and peace of his own beloved moor. He was aware of the blue eyes searching his face.

'That would be very kind of you,' said Dettner.

'You've got some walking shoes? I'll collect you at ten hundred, then.'

The aquatic sports, strictly confined to those who had not been libertymen that morning, were a great success and went on until evening quarters. In the meantime Peter made his arrangements for Saturday.

After Colours in the morning, Peter lingered on the quarterdeck to finalise the provisions for his absence. Those who wished to attend the cricket match had been approved shore leave from 1400 to 1800 hours only, everyone to be mustered for the Royal Marines band Beating the Retreat.

'Should be all right, sir,' said Bunny Hare. 'Can we reach you at all if anything should crop up?'

'You can leave a message for me at home. I'll drop in there during the afternoon. And I'll be back by eighteen hundred hours.'

'Right, sir.'

Bunny was watching the ship ahead of them and Peter turned to see what was holding his attention. On the quarterdeck, the *Seehaven*'s officers were indulging in physical exercise, led by their Captain, all garbed in the shortest of blue shorts and nothing else. Peter chuckled and picked up his binoculars.

'Strength through joy,' he murmured. 'I must say they look fit, though.'

He went below to change into civvies – corduroys and a hacking jacket with stout, brown shoes – and felt happy that he was going to the Moor and would be calling in at his home.

The car he had borrowed had been waiting overnight on the quayside and, remembering the German destroyer's arrival, he pulled up at the foot of their brow at precisely ten o'clock. The sharp salutes of the Officer of the Watch and the Quartermaster at the head of it, heralded the appearance of their Captain who, bareheaded, acknowledged them with a nod and came down to the car.

'This is good,' he said as he slid into the passenger seat. 'Is it yours?'

'No. My Navigator lives in Seahaven so I gave him twenty-four hours' leave from eighteen hundred last night to go and potter in his garden, provided I had his car.'

Dettner laughed and settled back to watch the scenery. Like Peter he was wearing a lightweight tweed jacket with cavalry twill slacks and highly-polished brogues. Like Bunny, Peter decided this was no impecunious naval officer – the clothes looked suspiciously Savile Row.

'Have you been to England much?' he asked.

'I have come to London sometimes. But not to the West Country before.'

They had left Seahaven now and were negotiating narrow lanes and Peter gave his attention to his driving. His companion seemed quite content to watch the passing scenery without conversation apart from asking about some big house they passed or what town or village they were going through.

Then they reached some flat, open moorland and sped along a narrow road flanked by coarse grass and gorse bushes until Peter turned the car up a short gravelled lane to a gate. Dettner slipped out of the car and opened it before Peter said a word and they drove on across the downland to a ridge above a swift flowing silver stream. Here, Peter drew up.

'Now, we walk,' he said.

In front of them, across the stream, the tors rose in majesty, brown and green and purple, dotted with sheep and the small, brown ponies. They got out of the car and a soft moorland breeze brought the scent of many things to them and, in the silence, the sound of the baaing sheep, a shrill call from a pony stallion to his mares and the unceasing babble of the stream over its gravelly bed.

Peter watched his companion. He could almost see the peace of the moor enfolding him. Then Dettner drew a deep breath and nodded towards the tor.

'Up there?' he said.

'Yes. Are you game?' said Peter.

'Game?'

'Ready to try it.' Peter locked the car. 'Eight hundred and something feet above sea level.'

They crossed the stream by the narrow footbridge and followed the sheep tracks up the side of the tor. Gorse, bracken and ling studded their way and the odd, twisted, stunted tree. They made the top together in silence and breathing deeply. A great granite outcrop crowned the top and Dettner leaned against the rock and stared around. In every direction the moor lay spread about him. The car parked below was a tiny speck and the road they had come by was barely visible. Peter, drawing in the clean, soft air through his mouth, did not speak. He was aware of the effect of the moor on someone who had not known it before. He was glad that it was showing its smiling face to this new visitor. The wild, grim face that it could show was not what he had wanted.

'So beautiful,' murmured Dettner. 'It is so beautiful and we shall spoil it.'

'Oh, no,' said Peter, quietly. 'You cannot spoil it. This will always be here.'

Dettner straightened.

'Where now?' he said.

Peter looked at his watch.

'Lunch, I think,' he said.

They lunched at a moorland inn on beer and ploughman's. The *Fregatten-Kapitän* insisted on paying because, he said, the Consul had given him English money and apart from sufficient for the church collection tomorrow he must spend it. Peter grinned and did not argue.

He did not warn Dettner that they were stopping off at his home and the man read the lettering on the granite gate posts curiously.

'Greystone Manor – where is this?'

'I told you I lived on Dartmoor,' said Peter. He stopped the car before the door. 'Come on. My father is ex-Navy. He'll be pleased to see you.'

The door was open and as they went towards it a small and extremely unsteady toddler in a blue romper suit came out. He blundered into Dettner's legs and the man bent and picked him up, laughing. The two women who followed the child out regarded him appreciatively for a moment, then the elder held out her arms and he put the child into them.

'This is *Fregatten-Kapitän* Dettner,' said Peter. 'My wife – and son. And my sister, Morwenna.'

Dettner took the hand that Peter's wife held out to him and touched it to his lips. Morwenna's he bowed over, slightly. Peter concealed a smile.

'Where's Dad, Kate?' he asked.

'In the garden,' she said. 'Shall we go through?'

Rear-Admiral Sillifant had only comparatively recently retired and found time could hang heavily. He had never had time to apply himself to the management of his family estate and he did not propose now to interfere with the work of a perfectly satisfactory estate manager. He was browsing through his newspaper at the garden table and rose to greet the visitor interestedly.

'*Fregatten-Kapitän*,' he repeated. 'That's Commander, isn't it? It's a good life, the Navy. Looks as though I might be back in it next year.'

'I am afraid it does, sir,' said Dettner.

'Well – thank God you've admitted it,' said the Admiral. 'Most people say "Oh, it won't come to that"!'

They stayed for a quick cup of tea and then set off again for Seahaven.

'This has been a wonderful day, Commander,' said Dettner as they neared the port. 'I am grateful.'

'Well – I wanted you to admire Dartmoor,' murmured Peter.

3

Fregatten-Kapitän Dettner was not a sentimental man; he might even have been described as hard. He had lived a hard life from early boyhood; at the Naval Academy and in the training ships, both sail and steam. But the British Commander's action in taking him to Dartmoor and then to his family home had touched him.

He sat down on his bunk, unbuttoning his shirt, and thought back over the day: the quiet little villages with gardens full of flowers, the deep unbounded beauty of the moor. The warm, soft little body of the British Commander's son in his hands: that was something he had not had time for, marriage and children. The bright sunshine, the soft, scented moorland air had made him sleepy.

When his steward came in to lay out his mess undress, *Fregatten-Kapitän* Dettner was sound asleep on his bunk.

The sound of the Royal Marine band marching down from the town square, where they had debussed, to the dockyard was just making itself heard as Dettner and his Number One, *Kapitän-Leutnant* Horst Pfeiffer, both immaculate in mess kit, made their way along the quay from one ship to the other where they were welcomed aboard by Bunny Hare and taken up to the open bridge. Pfeiffer was a sturdy, young man with a round, open face and a cheerful, slightly naïve manner but – as his counterpart Number One knew from their liaison at the sports – a very alert and efficient officer. His command of English was not always sure but Dettner was swift to translate for him and get him out of difficulty.

The remaining officers and men of both ships were mustered and the Colours parties were on the quarterdecks. Not strictly orthodox, thought Peter, but they would not normally be having a ceremonial like this and could only try to work in conjunction with Seahaven's wishes and have their 'Sunset' rather early. The July evening was still bright and the Civic party and other spectators were basking in the sunshine on the dockside. Peter hoped he had not been expected to entertain them in the wardroom.

The Royals now swung into view, marching as only they could, the tune changing as they came to the wharves and began the ceremonial, parading up and down between the two ships. At the appropriate point the two ensigns were gently lowered, the officers saluting, and the band came to a halt. The Mayor made a request to the bandmaster and both national anthems were played, throughout which all officers stood rigidly at the salute. The band then marched off and the spectators and dignitaries began to disperse.

'Side party, Number One,' snapped Peter. 'The Mayor's coming over.'

He, together with his German guests, followed Bunny more slowly to arrive on the quarterdeck to greet the Mayor and Mayoress and the local Police Superintendent, who had by then reached the top of the brow.

'Welcome aboard,' said Peter, pleased to see that the Mayor had doffed his hat, the Superintendent had saluted and the Mayoress had inclined her head to the now non-existent crucifix on the quarterdeck. 'Will you come below for a drink?'

'No, thanks, Captain,' said the Mayor. 'We just wanted the chance to say thank you to you and the – er – *Kapitän* for coming and taking part in our little celebrations. We shall see you at St Ordulph's tomorrow but there may not be time then. Now, we have to go and entertain the Marine bandsmen. Aren't they splendid?'

'Magnificent,' agreed Peter, casting a sad glance at his naked ensign staff. 'We have been delighted to be here. I am sure *Fregatten-Kapitän* Dettner will agree with me.'

'We have had much pleasure,' said Dettner. 'And my officers greatly enjoyed the cricket match, this afternoon.'

With much handshaking and saluting, the civic party withdrew to their cars and Peter said to Dettner, in disbelief, 'Did they? Enjoy the match?'

'They told me,' said Dettner, straightfaced, 'that the deckchairs were very comfortable and they slept all the way through. Then they had cream tea. What is that?'

'Cream teas,' said Peter, chuckling. 'A Devon delicacy of splits with jam and clotted cream. Come below.'

Bunny drew him aside as they got to the wardroom.

'So's I can put it around,' he said. 'How far do we go, after dinner?'

Peter reflected on some of the more rowdy evenings in the mess.

'Play it by ear,' he said. 'But I think softly, softly. I don't want to see bow ties and studs sculling around.'

'Very good, sir. Preserve the dignity, eh?'

Peter nodded and joined his guests. Both, of course, knew most of the other officers and both were quite outgoing. Pfeiffer's uncertain English and his C.O.'s constant rescue of him from disaster added to the hilarity and, after dinner, the question of what happened next did not arise. The stocky *Kapitän-Leutnant* spied the piano in a corner of the wardroom and begged permission which was granted immediately. He had an excellent repertoire of bawdy songs, ballads, musical comedy numbers and shanties and picked up very quickly a tune hummed to him and, since all self-respecting wardrooms love a sing-song, the evening sped rousingly on its way.

It broke up at midnight when Dettner persuaded a slightly inebriated pianist to his feet and instructed him to make polite farewells to his hosts. It was not surprising, Peter thought, that Pfeiffer was well away since he had been plied with drink to keep him going. He also noted that Dettner was stone-cold sober.

The ships' companies, 25 strong each, marched to St Ordulph's Church in the centre of the town in the morning. The ten officers were given a long central pew behind the town representatives and dignitaries, the men on either side of the church in side pews, although both first lieutenants had made sure they were under the control of stalwart Chiefs and P.O.s.

The two C.O.s, since they had entered the pew from opposite aisles, found themselves together in the centre and were able to exchange brief comments before the service began.

'No Pfeiffer?' said Peter, remembering that young man's enthusiastic singing.

'No – he is Roman Catholic,' said Dettner. 'So I have left him in charge.'

'You still have – religions?' Peter did not know how to put it.

'Under Hitler?' Dettner's quiet voice was unexpectedly bitter. 'Yes – we are not all quite Godforsaken.'

He stood up and Peter quickly followed as the vicar came down between the choir stalls.

Dettner also had an excellent singing voice and was not ashamed to use it, Peter found, and the seamen on either side of the church swelled the hymns in deep-throated unison.

As the Mayor had foreseen, there was no time for farewells and thanks after the service. The ships' companies were formed up and marched off and at the dockside were dismissed to dinner. Having seen their men aboard in the company of the other three officers, Peter and Bunny walked along to the German destroyer. Dettner and Pfeiffer were awaiting them.

The lay-out below, the British officers found, was similar to their own ships. The eating and leisure halves of the wardroom were spacious and the main difference in the hospitality was the presence of schnapps on the drink list. Three of the other officers besides Dettner spoke good English and several of the others managed some, like Pfeiffer, so a fair amount of translating went on through lunch. Afterwards, in an armchair in the sitting end, with a cup of excellent coffee, Peter asked Dettner how he felt about the visit.

'It went off well. We did not, I think, do everything by the book but if they were happy, that is all right. But – what difference will it make?'

'You mean war is inevitable?'

'I mean, my friend, that next year we shall be enemies.'

Some of the officers were leaving the wardroom. Occasionally one came in and reported to the Captain. They were obviously making preparations to sail and Peter caught Bunny's eye. At present Dettner seemed in no hurry and was content to leave things to Pfeiffer. Peter stood up and Dettner rose with him.

'Thank you, Captain,' Peter said as Bunny joined him. 'I have enjoyed meeting you and your officers. I wish I could say I hope we meet again.'

They both knew that it was almost certain that to meet again would be in battle.

Back aboard *Curre*, they watched *Seehaven* prepare for sea, the men take up stations for leaving harbour, the moorings cast off from the English dockside, the ensign descend from the staff and break out at the peak, the sound of the engine room telegraphs, the soft froth of water at the stern.

Bunts, with them on the bridge, said, 'She's signalling, sir. "Goodbye and many thanks".'

'Right – Reply –' Oh, God, what? 'Reply "Godspeed."' Peter turned. 'Be ready to slip at sixteen hundred hours, Number One.'

He went below to his cabin. He felt like weeping at the sheer futility of it all.

Peter reported to Captain (D) the next morning.

'Well, Peter,' said Captain Chalmers. 'We've had a message from Seahaven's Mayor and from the Police Super. I gather both were very pleased.'

'We didn't quite keep to KR&AIs*, sir but I think they were happy.'

'And the row in the town square. I gather you broke that up?'

'I didn't have a lot to do with it, sir. Captain Dettner called his men off and, thank God, ours held back.'

'What did you make of Dettner? An interesting character?'

'Yes. A complex character. One to be reckoned with if we go to war.'

'Yes.' Chalmers picked a paper from his desk. 'I've got a summary of his career to date. Interested?'

'Yes, sir.' Peter settled back in his chair, his cap on his knee. 'He's quite well-heeled, I'd say.'

'Should be. His father's Albrecht Dettner, owns the U.O. shipping line – Ulsdorf und Ost – operates from Fremenshaven. Hans Gerhardt is his only son, born 1905. General cargo line, very important to Germany in the last war. When all the seamen were taken for the U-boats in 1917, Albrecht sent his son to sea.'

*King's Regulations and Admiralty Instructions – the Paymaster's bible

'Twelve?' said Peter, stunned. 'To sea in a cargo ship at twelve?'

'Don't forget we had snotties at sea then, aged thirteen and fourteen,' said Chalmers, cynically. 'Anyway, a lot of the U.O. vessels went for reparations and so on at the end of the war but the old man built up again. He used to run short-haul cargoes to the Port of London in the twenties and the son used to sail with them. We left them a nucleus of naval ships, as I expect you know, and fifteen thousand men, so young Hans went as a naval cadet. In 1927 he was *Leutnant zur See* and he also took his Master Mariner's ticket. To celebrate he took extended leave and went to Calcutta in one of his father's ships – as Master.'

'As Master,' repeated Peter. 'At twenty-two?'

'And with God knows what sort of crew. The dregs of Bremen?' Chalmers referred to the paper again. 'After that he seems to have settled down as a good little naval officer. Some time at the Admiralty in Berlin, a year or so as a Flag Lieutenant, a stint in heavy cruisers and, as we know, in the *Admiral Graf Spee* when she came to the Coronation Review last year. After that trip he went to destroyers. Of course he's younger than both Langsdorff and Lindemann but he's heading in the same direction, I'd say.'

'You have a good informant, sir?'

'Oh, we keep CVs on the bright boys. I expect they've got one on you.'

Peter managed to look sceptically flattered. But his mind was on the top of a tor and a man awestruck by the beauty and frightened for its safety. A man who had laughed as he picked up a wriggling toddler.

4

The house at Ulsdorf had originally stood in quite an extensive garden but gradually the repair yard had spread from the river and it stood now with only a lane between it and the office block on the edge of the yard. It was a square, uncompromising looking house of three storeys, but, within, reflected the acquired wealth of its owner and master.

Albrecht Dettner had been a handsome, upstanding man in his younger days but good living was swelling his flesh and the unchecked gratification of his own desires had imprinted impatience and arrogance on his face. Unchecked in all ways but one. When his son came into his office soon after the triumphant invasion of Poland had been announced over the radio, he looked at his uniform with a sneer on his face.

'Still in your pretty boy suit,' he said. 'If you'd stayed with my ships you'd be wearing four rings on your sleeve, not three.'

'I wore those when I was twenty-two,' said his son. 'Where would I have gone from there?'

Albrecht snorted contemptuously.

'Are you off to war? Are the British going to fight?'

'I expect so. I report to Wilhelmshaven tomorrow.'

'Destroyer?'

'No. A cruiser.'

'*Graf Spee*'s sailed. A fine ship. Pity you didn't go back to her.'

Hans Dettner did not answer. He looked out of the window which gave a view across the yard to the river. Two of the cargo ships were alongside with the buff and black funnels of the U.O. line. He had no desire to repeat his first voyage as Master of one of them which had been done out of sheer bravado and a desire to shut off his father's constant criticism of the way things were done in the navy. The thought of the coming war filled him with horror and the possibility of a repetition of the conclusion of it and another Treaty of Versailles was not to be borne. That it would be over – if, of course, the British declared war which was not generally considered likely – by Christmas with a resounding victory, an overrunning of France and an invasion of England, he did not believe.

He wondered what war would bring to that sunlit house on Dartmoor. The father, the Rear Admiral, would go happily back to the Navy and no doubt die bravely as a Convoy Commodore. The daughter would join the women's service and meet many fine Naval officers and get married – as his own sister had done, but her husband was in the Army and had marched into Poland. And she, now pregnant, would remain at home like the English Commander's wife with her child and suffer the privations of civilians.

Hans Dettner, heavy-hearted, turned from the window and picked up his cap.

'I shall see you this evening?' he asked, politely.

'Yes. You're going back to the house? I've a lot to do here but tell your mother I'll be in for dinner.'

The son left the shipper's office. He did not want to go back to the house. He would have reported to the Naval Base immediately if he could but his orders gave the time and date to be a.m. Saturday, 2 September 1939 and that was when he would report. He crossed the road from the yard and entered the house.

Its furnishings were too familiar to him for either liking or disliking. They were, presumably, what his parents had chosen when the business prospered and he had grown up with them, had left on his voyages and come back to them and would now be going again but whether or not to come back he did not know.

His mother and sister were sitting in the garden at the back of the house away from the yard and again his thoughts were taken back to the garden on Dartmoor, over a year ago now and the elderly man eager to get back into harness and the two young women with the toddler, who had sat on his father's knee while they dispensed tea in delicate china.

Frau Dettner was not a big woman. From her came her son's

slender build. She came of an old Prussian family and her back was as rigid as her philosophy. Her daughter, Isolde, took after her father, a bigger woman and even bigger now and fretful with her advancing pregnancy and the worry of her husband's departure into Poland.

'Hans,' Frau Dettner said. 'Have you seen your father?'

'Yes, Mother. He will be in for dinner.'

'Good. Now, sit down and have some coffee.'

They were having coffee and cakes and he obeyed her and took a cup of coffee. His feelings of wretchedness and almost homesickness increased. He wanted to be away to sea. But it was not the salt-laden sea air that he could smell but the soft, sweet-scented air of Dartmoor.

And there, over in Devon, Peter was saying goodbye to Kate and Morwenna and two-year-old John. He was also going to a fresh appointment in a big new fleet destroyer unlike his little Hunt class *Curre* and his father was already in London, badgering old shipmates for a job.

They knew *Graf Spee* had sailed from Wilhelmshaven and was already in the Atlantic but so far no declaration of war had been made. They had to wait until Sunday for the fateful words from the Prime Minister: '...a state of war exists between us and Germany.'

Morwenna had already sent in her application to join the WRNS. She was driving Peter to Plymouth that afternoon where he would catch the train to London and from there the night train up north.

They stood on the platform before the train left and said meaningless things like, 'I'll be in the WRNS before you get leave, I expect'; 'Take care of yourself'; 'Give my love to Dad – hope he's got a job'; 'Don't wait' and 'I'd better go' right up to the time the guard's whistle shrilled and they had a quick hug and Peter swung into the train and watched the platform and the station and his sister slide away. He sat down wondering if and when he would see them again.

The casualties of war, big and little, mounted on both sides. For Hans Dettner the scuttling of the *Graf Spee* and the suicide of Langsdorff, the deaths of Lütjens and Lindemann with *Bismarck*, the sinking of the destroyer *Seehaven* with all her company including Horst Pfeiffer. For Peter Sillifant the torpedoing of *Royal Oak* in Scapa, the destruction of *Hood* and the loss of the little Hunt class *Curre* escorting Atlantic convoys.

More personally, Dettner's light cruiser and his destroyer screen took part in the battle for Norway and thereafter operated mainly in the North Sea, spending some time holed up in various fjords, venturing up to the Arctic Circle to harry convoys. A sharp engagement with some of the escorts put his ship in dock and himself in hospital and when he came out after a relatively brief stay he went commerce raiding with the *Admiral Scheer*.

Peter, also on Atlantic convoy duty, witnessed the end of *Curre* and picked up the few survivors. In 1942, his father, having had two ships sunk beneath him, as Commodore, was invalided out of the Service to his great chagrin and having no success in agitating for a shore job retired to Greystone Manor where he was cosseted by Kate and admired by his young grandson. Morwenna was now a cypher officer on the staff of C-in-C Western Approaches in Liverpool.

In 1943, Peter also lost his ship in the Atlantic and found himself in London, visiting his old Captain (D) now Rear Admiral Chalmers, at Queen Anne's Mansions.

Having discussed Peter's new appointment Chalmers remarked, 'By the way, I heard some news about an old friend of yours – *Kapitän zur See* Dettner has just taken command of a heavy cruiser, *Prinz Ludwig*, and will no doubt be pursuing his career as a commerce raider.'

'Dettner? Still surviving then, sir?'

'Very much so.'

In 1944, just after the Normandy landings, Peter got home on a brief leave while some much needed patching was done to his ship and received a guarded letter from Morwenna which indicated she was going to sea as part of the Naval signals team seconded to troopships. The name, she said obliquely, was a bit like his little, pre-war destroyer. This, decided Peter, must mean the S.S. *Curie*, a French liner destined for South Atlantic passages before she had been 'liberated' after the French capitulation. She would probably be taking German prisoners across to Canada and bringing

Canadian troops back to swell the invasion forces. Quite a lot of troops, thought Peter, since she was a ship of some 40,000 tons. He debated it with his father.

'A fast ship,' said the Rear Admiral. 'She'll go alone, not in convoy.'

So Peter returned to his own war but not to his old ship. His promotion came through and as Captain (D) he took over the flotilla.

Hans Dettner, roving the Atlantic in *Prinz Ludwig*, was well aware of the passage of the S.S. *Curie* and the passengers she carried. He let her complete the voyage west with the prisoners and caught her as she headed towards the Azores on her return trip, filled with the troops who were to back up the armies now advancing towards his country.

She was armed, as a Defensively Equipped Merchant Ship and the solitary gun was manned by DEMS gunners. Against *Prinz Ludwig*'s crashing broadside she didn't have a chance. However, before Dettner completed her destruction with torpedoes, she got off an SOS giving her position and saying, 'Under attack by surface raider.'

Dettner and his Number One, *Fregatten-Kapitän* Kassel, watched through glasses as the great liner sank, eventually plunging stern-first in a great welter of fume and spray. Then there was only the wreckage left on the heaving sea and the bobbing heads and waving arms. Hundreds of them. Dettner let his glasses fall to his chest and turned away. For a moment he pressed a hand to his mouth as if he felt sick. They were soldiers. They were coming to invade Germany. They were men.

But they had given away his presence and he had to get away from the scene as fast as he could. Below, he could see some of the men loitering near the boats as if expecting the call for rescue boats to be lowered.

'Full ahead, all,' said Dettner to the Officer of the Watch.

He didn't look back at the black dots in the water. He hoped that any ships who had heard the SOS were not too far away.

5

For his successful attack on the troopship S.S. *Curie*, resulting in the total loss of her passengers and crew, Dettner received the Knight's Cross to add to his Iron Cross.

Less than a year later he was in the South Atlantic meeting with his supply ship when the news came through on the radio of the death of Hitler and the reluctant assumption of power by *Grandadmiral* Dönitz. Then the bald announcement that all armed forces had surrendered. This was followed by the order to all German ships at sea to make for their home ports or to an Allied port, whichever was the nearest. The Captain of the supply ship decided he would make for the Falklands and surrender there. Dettner called his officers and crew together on the quarterdeck. He didn't say much but he gave them a choice.

'Where you will,' he said. 'We have fuel and food. Falklands, Cape Town, Australia... Home.'

There was no dissent. So he called Kassel, the Navigating Officer, and the Signals Officer to him.

'Work out the date and time of arrival, Pilot,' he said. 'Make this signal to Admiralty, London. "*Prinz Ludwig* proceeding Wilhelmshaven ETA date and time." Thank you, gentlemen.'

He went down to his cabin and got his steward to remove the Nazi eagle and swastika from his uniforms.

In Admiralty, London, an Admiral and a Rear Admiral sitting together in an office off the Operations Room had a chuckle over the radio message.

'He will do it, won't he?' said the white-haired Admiral.

'Oh, he'll do it, all right,' said Rear Admiral Chalmers.

'Probably the best place to have him, anyway,' said the

Admiral. 'It would be a nuisance if he went and scuttled her in the Falklands or somewhere. You'd best pick him up when he gets North of Scotland and escort him the rest of the way.'

'North of Scotland?' said Chalmers. 'Suppose he comes through the Channel? He's got enough cheek.'

'The English Channel? Better pick him up off Finisterre, then.' The Admiral started to laugh again. '"Proceeding Wilhelmshaven." Bloody sauce!'

Prinz Ludwig was duly intercepted as she approached Brest and boarded by an RN Commander, a CPO and six ratings.

'I take it you're going the shortest way, Captain,' said the Commander in Dettner's cabin.

'Yes, of course.' Dettner glanced through the scuttle as the escorting destroyers took up position. 'I would have got there without all this, you know, Commander.'

'I'm sure you would, sir. We just thought we'd like to see you in.'

Dettner laughed. He took up a bottle.

'Will you drink with me? It is my fortieth birthday today.'

'With pleasure. May you have happier returns than this one.'

'Thank you.' Dettner gave him a glass. 'Tell me, do you know a Commander – or perhaps Captain now – Peter Sillifant?'

'Yes, I do.' The Commander emptied his glass and put it down on the table. 'He's Captain (D) now.' He paused and added, deliberately, 'His sister was a cypher officer on board the S.S. *Curie*.'

He watched the colour drain from the German Captain's face.

'There were women on board?' he said, almost inaudibly.

'There were five Wrens – coders and cypherers – and a number of Canadian forces women.'

Dettner closed his eyes, leaning back in his chair. He saw the bobbing heads, the waving arms. He saw the two women and the child at the sunlit door. When he looked up, the Commander was standing, looking down at him with a queer compassion in his eyes.

'Did you know Captain Sillifant's sister, sir?'

Dettner got up. He went to the scuttle and stared out.

'I met his family once – in 1938,' he said. 'You bring me a cruel birthday present, Commander.'

'I'm sorry, sir. Perhaps I should not have told you. It – wouldn't have made any difference, though, would it?'
'No. No, I had to sink her. I had to leave them.'
'We've all been there,' said the Commander, gently. 'I'll go up top now, sir. Thanks for the drink.'

He tucked his cap under his arm and went out. His CPO was with the German sentry outside in the Captain's flat. He nodded to him and went up the ladder to the bridge.

At present, all was proceeding as normal, the ship's routine continuing and discipline maintained. As they approached the harbour with the crew lined up at harbour stations, with the forecastle and quarterdeck parties in position, the Captain on the bridge, some of the horror of the situation began to hit them.

They saw the recent devastation of the port, the gangs of men clearing rubble, the British khaki, the British Navy sailors on the dockside.

The Commander, on the bridge beside Dettner, marvelled at his fortitude as he brought the great ship safely into her berth, awaited the calls from the mooring parties and rang off engines. He had spoken to Dettner earlier about the full extent of the situation that awaited them and the Captain had called for the whole ship's company to muster aft, immediately on docking.

As *Prinz Ludwig* settled to rest against her fenders, the men were already coming aft and forming up in their divisions and the Commander looked at Dettner, his heart wrenched with pity at the knowledge of what the man had now to do. He saw him visibly pull himself together as he made to follow his officers down to the quarterdeck.

Ex-*Kapitän zur See* Hans Dettner looked over the assembled company for a while in silence. Then he began.

'You asked me to bring you home,' he said, 'and I have done so. You can see that there is much to be done here. I am told that you can obtain work by cooperating with the Occupying Forces, clearing the damage or in the dockyard and naval offices. Certain of you, key men, will remain aboard to hand over stores and equipment. But you understand, there is no longer a German navy. You are instructed to remove all badges of rank from your uniform and go home. You will be given travel passes at the dockyard office. I, now, have no rank. I no longer have the right to command you. So I ask you, please, to leave our ship quietly and in good order. May God go with you.'

His voice was clear and unfaltering but as he turned to go below, the British Commander could see the brimming tears in his eyes.

Dettner and the Pilot remained aboard for a few days, handing over books and charts and overseeing the inventories of stores and equipment. Then, at last, the Commander found himself alone again in the Captain's day cabin, the ship strangely silent and empty, the cabin stripped of personal things, Dettner's steward just removing his suitcases.

'What will happen to *Prinz Ludwig*, now?' Dettner asked him, taking up the whisky bottle.

'We may take her. Or she could go to France or Poland, so on, as part of the reparations.'

'Not Russia, I hope,' said Dettner with a sigh and gave the Commander a glass. 'Should I have scuttled her? I wanted to get my men home. But what have they come to?'

'You have brought them home, sir,' said the Commander. 'Now it is up to you all to rebuild your country. We shall help you but it will be hard.'

'Yes. I was thirteen last time. I can remember – it was hard.' He picked up the bottle. 'Just enough left,' he said, topping up their glasses. 'What do we drink to?'

'I think – just that this will never happen again.'

'That – yes.'

'Right, sir.' The Commander stood up. 'I've arranged a car for you to take you home.' He knew only too well the heart-tearing wrench it was for the man to leave his ship and thought for a moment to leave him to himself for the last few minutes. But Dettner rose, threw one searching glance around and went up with him to the quarterdeck.

The car was waiting, a German driver at the wheel and an armed seaman standing by the door. Dettner's steward, his uniform badgeless, had stowed the cases and was also waiting. He was a local man and had found employment in the dockyard stores office. He saluted and shook hands with his ex-Captain and held the car door open for him.

'Thank you, Commander,' said Dettner. 'You have been very understanding.'

He got into the car, the sentry took his seat and they drove off.

In distance, it was not a long journey but they had to go cross-country from Varel and the roads were poor and had suffered from the bombing. They had to wait to cross the Weser but eventually drew up in the lane between the two buildings. The house was still untouched, the yard had suffered some damage and was empty and silent.

The driver got out and put the two suitcases down on the doorstep. The armed, belted and gaitered seaman also got out, to Dettner's mild surprise.

'There you are, home, sir,' he said, with gruff kindness. 'Good luck.'

Shattered, Dettner watched them go. They were his last link with his ship, with his old life, the only life he had wanted since his cadet days. What lay ahead he could not visualise. What employment he could find, what money he could earn, he did not know. Whom to approach he did not know. His orders had always come from higher authority; he had not had to seek them out. But now? There would be a British Naval HQ presumably and a Military Governor – Civil Authorities? Resettlement offices?

He opened the door, dumped his suitcases in the hall and went to find his family. They were all in his mother's drawing room and the collective, accusing faces were like a body blow. Albrecht Dettner was obviously a broken man: his flesh had shrunk and he cringed in his chair beside his ramrod stiff wife, Hanna. By the window, a gaunt-looking Isolde had her five-year-old son on her lap.

'Well, Hans?' said Hanna. 'I hope you have brought some rations with you. Otherwise you will have to make do with bean soup.'

He was silent, mortified. In the agony of losing *Prinz Ludwig* he had not given a thought to the household at Ulsdorf. His father should still have been capable of providing for them but, apparently, the second loss of his fleet had destroyed him.

'Have you brought me something?' whined the child.

'No. No, I have nothing. I have eaten. I do not need anything.'

Hans Dettner escaped to his bedroom and sat down on the bed. He found he was trembling. This was more awful than he could ever have imagined.

6

As he breakfasted alone the following morning, off black bread and acorn coffee, only his second meal in the last 24 hours, ex-Captain Dettner thought bitterly of yesterday's breakfast on board *Prinz Ludwig* and of all the stores he had signed away there.

His destination this morning was Fremenshaven, his purpose to find work. Since no one was likely to offer him a job as ship's master he had put on casual clothes and shoes stout enough for the walk there and back.

By mid-morning, having been directed and redirected from one office to another he fetched up before the desk of a C.W.O. R.N. who was backed up by a P.O. Writer. The Warrant Officer indicated a chair and looked him over. Dettner wondered what he saw: a quite well-nourished-still man of 40, above medium height but slim-built with the unblemished hands of a non-manual worker.

Commissioned Warrant Officer Martin, as proclaimed by the wooden plaque on his desk, signed to his Writer who went to a filing cabinet and took out a buff folder. It was labelled 'Dettner, U.O. Shipping Line'. Martin opened it and browsed through it for a few moments. Then he looked up.

'You need work and rations for your dependants?' he said. 'What dependants do you claim?'

'Parents and a sister with a young child.'

Martin looked down at the open folder.

'Your father is only sixty-five,' he said. 'Capable of work, surely? And your sister could do a useful job in the canteens. The child could be cared for by his grandmother. So – they are not really all dependants, are they?'

Dettner said nothing. He saw the crushed figure of Albrecht, the idle Isolde. In the end, because he was literate and numerate, the W.O. directed him to a job checking and listing stores. Because it meant a small wage and the right to draw rations, he did not demur. At least, all the rations could go to the household. He could make do with a midday meal at the canteen or with soup and bread from the NAAFI vans. He got up to go and find his new place of work.

As he opened the door he heard Martin say, 'That was the C.O. of *Prinz Ludwig* – the bastard who sank the troopship and left 'em all to drown.'

The P.O. laughed softly.

'How are the mighty fallen,' he said.

Hans Dettner stuck his office work for three months, walking there and back each day, getting leaner and harder. Then Isolde heard that her husband was being repatriated. He had been a Major on Paulus's staff and a prisoner in Russia since Paulus's surrender. He was reported to have severe frostbite and was unlikely to be fit for some time. Ex-Captain Dettner, shouldering the new responsibility, applied for a job on a harbour tug. As manual work, it would command better rations. So, as winter descended he took up his new situation as deckhand on a tug moving wrecks or shifting shipping around the harbour.

Because his hands were still too soft to handle ropes and wires without bleeding and because the waters of the harbour were obscenely polluted, he took to wearing gloves and the other deckhands found this amusing. But their jesting was not too cruel until one day, as 1946 moved into its second month, one of the hands discovered that the man whom they only knew as Hans, had once commanded the heavy cruiser *Prinz Ludwig*. Then, their mockery tore him apart.

The temporary Harbour Master, a bearded RNR lieutenant-commander, was merciful and called him into his office.

'I think enough is enough, Dettner,' he said. 'I knew there was a Dettner yard upriver but I did not know who you were until the men started getting at you.'

'The bastard who sank the *Curie*,' said Dettner.

The Harbour Master contemplated him.

'That, yes,' he said. 'I have had to leave men to die in the sea because it was more important to depth-charge the U-boat than to pick them up. Don't think you're alone with your nightmares.'

'I am sorry.'

'But that's not what your fellows are mocking you for, is it? It's because you were an officer and are now without rank. Yes?'

'Yes.'

'I see from your file that you hold a Master Mariner's ticket. Think you could handle an ocean-going tug?'

'You mean – as Master?'

'Yes, as Master.'

The job consisted mainly of towing vessels out to sea to be sunk in deep water or old merchantmen filled with the detritus of war to be consigned to the depths. On these occasions a RNVR lieutenant, an explosives expert, came out with the tug, boarded the doomed ship and placed his charges, then had to be taken off again, together with the small passage crew. The tug then stood by until the explosions tore the bottom out of the ship and she sank. Each position had to be accurately plotted and logged.

Through the winter months Dettner wore his old naval bridge coat or a leather jacket without rank badges and as the summer came was usually in shirt sleeves with an open collar. The only sign of his position was his gold-leafed skipper's cap.

Dettner and the expert, Lieutenant Conway RNVR, got to know each other very well. Conway had been on Special Ops in the Mediterranean for some time and he could talk long and amusingly about Greek and Albanian guerrillas. The dicey nature of his job had given him a blasé veneer but he was a serious and efficient young man. He and the unlikely tugmaster respected each other.

Towards the end of the summer, three old ships of the U.O. Line were due for demolition. They had been loaded with old shells, mines, rubble and rubbish, the nature of the cargo making it necessary to place the demolition charges with care. The first two were successfully disposed of, one in the morning, one in the afternoon of one day, the third to go the next morning. From each, there needed to be a quick getaway.

It was a fine, sunny day with only a gentle swell on the water but even so, with the tow cast off, it required constant helm and engine orders to keep the tug alongside the wallowing vessel without crashing into it. The passage crew, duties completed, came tumbling down the suspended ladder and timed their jumps on to the tug's deck, the last to descend being Conway who clambered up the bridge ladder, shouting.

'Sheer off – quick as you can. She's not too stable.'

Once on the bridge, the tug heading away from the cargo vessel, he looked down at the passage crew, standing below.

'Hullo!' he said. 'Where's the old man?'

Dettner looked at him and then down at the men below.

'Old man?' he repeated. 'They are the usual crew.'

'There was an old fellow there – came down with me. I sent him up to get off with the others. My God! – he's there on the bridge!'

Dettner took up his glasses and looked. At the salute on the bridge of his last old ship, stood Albrecht Dettner.

'What time?' asked his son without lowering his glasses.

'None,' said Conway, tersely. 'If we don't get a move on we'll go up too.'

Almost immediately the ship erupted and was rent by explosion after explosion, the shock waves rocking the massive tug as they reached her. Dettner lowered his glasses and turned away. Both Conway and the helmsman watched him.

'Did you know him?' asked Conway, after a moment.

No, thought Dettner, I didn't know him – I will never know him.

Aloud he said, 'It was my father.'

When the tug was safely berthed, Conway said awkwardly, 'There'll have to be an enquiry, of course – about how he got aboard and so on.'

'Yes.' Dettner picked up his leather jacket and put it on. 'We must go and report to the Harbour Master.'

He felt numbed. Why hadn't he known that it was something his father was likely to do? All the other U.O. ships had gone again for reparations. How obvious, with hindsight, that Albrecht would want to go with the last of them.

Having made their report, Dettner requested permission to go home to inform his mother. Conway and the Harbour Master Renfrew watched him go.

'For God's sake,' burst out Conway. 'That was his father! Has he no feelings?'

'No,' said the bearded Reservist. 'I shouldn't think he's got any left. Have you any idea what that man's been through?'

'Tell me, sir.'

'You heard of his message from the South Atlantic – to the Admiralty? Yes – he wanted to get his men home and has been reviled for not indulging in the national pastime of scuttling. The day after leaving his ship he was here in Fremenshaven, getting a job off that little squit Martin – who put him in stores, checking lists! Then he went as deckhand on the harbour tug until the others found out who he was and embarked on ex-officer baiting. So I rescued him from that and put him on the big tug. No – I shouldn't think he's got any feelings left, not outwardly. What's going on inside I'd not like to say.' He paused and added, slowly, 'Have you any idea what it's like to have to leave men to drown because you daren't stop to pick them up?'

'No, sir,' said Conway. 'But I take it you have – also.'

'Yes.' Renfrew was looking out of his office window. 'You don't forget them.'

Hans Dettner was walking home. What he was going to say he did not know.

When he got there only Isolde and the child with ex-Major Anton Wessel stretched on the sofa, were in the drawing room.

'Why are you back at this time?' asked Isolde.

He took a chocolate bar from his pocket and gave it to the child.

'Where is Mother?' he asked.

'In the garden. I think she's waiting for father to come back.'

Dettner went out and found the small, straight-backed woman walking up and down the path. He spoke her name and held out his hands.

She looked him up and down, ignoring his gesture.

'I know,' she said. 'He told me what he was going to do.'

His hands dropped.

'Why didn't you warn me?'

'You would not have let him do it.'

'You let me – blow up my father?'

'Will you tell your sister? Or shall I?'

He turned and left her, walking blindly out of the garden and back on the road to Fremenshaven. When he reached the tug he went up to the Captain's cabin abaft the bridge. He lay down on the bunk and curled up there, shivering. For some reason he thought of the Marines and 'Sunset'.

7

Captain Peter Sillifant had been pleased to find, when he had taken command of the cruiser *Moorhampton*, that his Executive Officer was Commander Jasper Hare. They had not served together since *Curre* and had a lot to catch up with in their off-duty moments.

Although Bunny Hare knew of the sinking of the S.S. *Curie* by the surface raider *Prinz Ludwig* he had not known that Morwenna Sillifant had perished with her. Peter, telling him, remembered his father standing by his mother's grave after the new inscription had been added to the stone: 'Also to the Memory of her Daughter Morwenna Jane, 1918–1944. Lost at Sea.'

Peter joined *Moorhampton* in early 1945. Bunny had already been aboard for six months and in August they sailed to Ceylon in time for the abrupt cessation of the Japanese war. For the next 18 months their beat lay between Colombo or Trincomalee and Singapore and Hong Kong. Despite the devastation of the latter two they found the commission a holiday after their joint experiences in the Atlantic, Mediterranean and on Russian convoys.

They were enjoying a yarn and a pre-lunch long, cool drink in Peter's forecabin peacefully at anchor, when the Signals Officer, cap tucked under his arm, came in.

'Signal, sir,' he said. 'Restricted. I've decoded it.'

'Thanks, Mike. Have a drink and sit down.' Peter took the signal pad and, after a moment, glanced at Bunny. 'It's from Chalmers: "Intercept and escort into Calcutta S.S. *Neumark*, carrying general cargo, under flag of convenience. Suspected gun-runner. Master is one Hans Dettner. Position so and so, ETA etc." Guns to Calcutta?'

'Nasty,' said Bunny. 'With Indian independence and the partition of the country. Calcutta will be near the border of East Pakistan, won't it?'

'H'm.' Peter considered. 'Mike, ask the Pilot to join us, would you?'

They were also joined a little later by Commander (E) and then Peter went ashore to clear his departure with the Staff Officer Operations who had also received the signal.

Hans Dettner had lost his tug when she was handed over to Poland and for a while he remained unemployed. Then a chit from W.O. Martin directed him to an office in Fremenshaven where he found a grey-haired man in civvies who introduced himself as Admiral Slater. Standing just behind him was a dark officer who was named as Commander Patel of the Royal Indian Navy.

'But we shall be free of the great British Raj,' he said with a fine display of white teeth. 'Then I shall be of the Pakistan Navy.'

'We have one of the U.O. Line ships,' interrupted the civilian-suited Admiral, 'which was taken over by the Nilssen Line of Denmark. She is loaded with general cargo and ready to sail for Calcutta. But the Master has been taken ill. Will you take her?'

'Many goods for the Independence celebrations, you understand,' put in the smiling Patel.

Dettner thought quickly. Anton Wessel was quite recovered and should be able to take on his own responsibilities now. As Martin had originally said there was no reason why Isolde should not earn money. For himself, the desire to get back to sea was overwhelming. He arranged a deal where he had an advance payment of wages for the voyage, the rest to be paid to his mother. Then he went home to pack a suitcase.

When he joined the ship, the S.S. *Neumark*, he found she was indeed ready to sail, port clearance already obtained. He had a mixed crew of Germans, Danes and Lascars and his Chief Officer and Chief Engineer both seemed efficient. It was not until they were two days out of port that he had time to study the cargo manifests.

There did not seem to be a lot that would contribute to the celebrations as the Indian naval officer had said. Some crates of children's toys, dolls' prams, push bikes, a number of crates of machine parts – nothing special, nothing significant. He asked the mate about them, since he had supervised the loading, but the man appeared quite satisfied that it was a normal cargo, destined for two separate importers in Calcutta. Dettner accepted it and settled down to the voyage.

He was using his old naval uniforms, stripped of medal ribbons and of all badges except the four plain gold rings on his sleeves. His cap badge was of the Nilssen Line. Though the ship still had the black and buff stack of the U.O. Line, the Nilssen house flag flew at her masthead, the port of registration had been obliterated and she sailed under the flag of Panama. These discrepancies worried Dettner but he could only trust in the good faith of the Admiral, Slater and of Nilssen, whom Albrecht Dettner had known, and the apparent complacency of the other officers.

So he was not unduly worried when the British cruiser, sleek and pale grey, intercepted him in the Bay of Bengal and politely enquired his identity, cargo and destination.

'S.S. *Neumark*, general cargo for Calcutta.'

'Straightforward enough,' said Peter to Bunny. 'All right. We'll let him go in and find out who is importing what.' He turned to the O.O.W. 'Tell him to proceed and we will accompany.' He picked up his glasses and focused on the wing of the cargo vessel's bridge where a white-uniformed figure waved an acknowledgement. Yes – the Master was 'one Hans Dettner'. He then busied himself with signals to Calcutta, to base and to Chalmers. Then they completed the voyage 'in company'.

'Reminded of anything?' he said to Bunny as they followed the *Neumark* to the jetty where she was to dock. Bunny grinned.

'A destroyer entering the Seahaven basin?' he said. 'I bet he won't do a right-about turn here, though.'

They chuckled in reminiscence together and proceeded to their own allotted berth on the other side of the jetty.

Cranes were already in position and hatch covers were coming off the *Neumark*'s holds when Dettner came down the gangway and turned shorewards. At the landward end of the jetty a police lieutenant in khaki shorts and shirt, together with two turbaned policemen stood watching impassively. They took no notice of Dettner, who went on to the shippers' offices.

The following morning he received a request to go to the British Consulate. It puzzled him a bit: there was no German Consul, of course, but he might have expected the Danish or Dutch to take over any consular business.

However, he proceeded as requested, noting as he went the cargo being piled on the dockside, cranes and winches busy, the First Mate checking out the crates as they came out of the hold, the Second supervising the handlers. The day was hot, stuffy and he wore white uniform trousers and a short-sleeved, open-collared shirt with the four gold rings on his shoulders.

He was admitted almost immediately into the Consul's office and did not at once recognise the two British officers sitting there. When he realised who they were, the swift surge of pleasure he felt was sharply obliterated by the memory of Sillifant's sister.

Peter, watching him come in, saw the pleasure in the keen, blue eyes, saw it die. Lean, brown face, leaner, harder now, fair hair, still plentiful, cap tucked under his arm, fresh whites, spotless shoes.

Peter got up and said to the Consul, 'This is Captain Dettner, Master of the S.S. *Neumark*, sir.'

'Please sit down, Captain Dettner,' said the Consul and paused to pick up a telephone which rang sharply. He listened for a moment, then said, 'Yes, I see. Thank you. Now, Captain Dettner, I believe you took over the *Neumark* at very short notice?'

'Yes.'

'What did you know of your cargo?'

'Only what was listed.'

'We received information that part of your cargo consisted of armaments. I have to tell you that the suspect crates have been broken open and the information has been found to be correct. The importer has been arrested. Do you tell me you knew nothing of this?'

Dettner could see the grey-haired self-styled Admiral and the dark-skinned naval officer. Ever been taken for a ride? He shook his head, numbly.

'Your ship and crew are under arrest. So, Captain Dettner, are you.'

The Consul pressed his bell and the police lieutenant in khaki shorts and shirt, his swagger cane under his arm, came in. At the door his two turbaned police constables waited. Dettner got up. He did not look at Peter and Bunny.

When prisoner and escort had gone, the Consul looked at the two British officers.

'I could do nothing else,' he said. 'The others will be all right, confined to the ship. But if your Admiral Chalmers can do anything I should get Captain Dettner out of Indian hands as soon as possible. A suspected gun-runner will not be popular. I will get on to Delhi.'

The flurry of signals emitting from *Moorhampton* and the telephone calls from the Consulate culminated in a coded message from Chalmers.

'Dettner is being handed over into your custody, p.m. today. *Moorhampton* to proceed to base to pick up sailing orders.'

Peter and Bunny were on the bridge, preparing to sail directly the prisoner was received, that afternoon. They felt no desire to linger a moment longer than necessary. There was a strange unrest about the place. They had heard tales of the massacre of muslims. They could see British residents preparing to leave – the end of the British Raj.

A jeep sped down the jetty and the Police Lieutenant jumped out and came smartly up the brow. Peter collected Bunny with a glance and went down the bridge ladder and on to the quarterdeck.

The policeman – a white officer – saluted him and said, 'I have a prisoner to give into your custody, sir.'

'Yes, I know,' said Peter and watched Dettner come on to the quarterdeck between the two Indians.

The deadened blue eyes told him that the man was almost at the limit of endurance. He had tried to salute the quarterdeck but he was handcuffed and barely managed it. His whites were crumpled and he had obviously slept in them if he had had any sleep. Peter turned on the white officer, furiously.

'Take those bloody cuffs off him,' he said, softly.

'When we've got him safely in your cells, sir,' said the lieutenant.

'You do not get him safely in my cells, Lieutenant,' said Peter with awful deliberation. 'He is now in my charge. Take those cuffs off him and get off my ship. Then have his personal possessions brought over here from the *Neumark*.'

Dettner waited silently while his chafed wrists were freed. Then he saluted Peter.

'Thank you, Captain,' he said.

'Come below,' said Peter, abruptly. 'Carry on, Commander. I'll be with you in five minutes.' In his day cabin he called his steward. 'Captain Dettner's things will be coming over from his ship directly. Put them in my guest cabin.' He turned to look at his prisoner. 'I have your parole I am sure. Now, I would suggest a bath and perhaps some tea. Petty Officer Clark will see to you.'

He went back up to the bridge. Dettner's silent apathy worried him. He saw the man's belongings brought to the brow by the two Indians and handed over to a seaman. Then he turned his attention to getting his ship out of harbour and to sea.

8

Moorhampton was well out into the bay when Peter and Bunny Hare went down to Peter's day cabin. He still felt anger at the Police Lieutenant's attitude. He called for 'Nobby' Clark who, when he came in, also appeared to be indignant.

'What's the matter, Clark?' said Peter. 'Where's Captain Dettner?'

'In 'is bunk an' asleep I 'ope, sir. 'E nearly went off in the bath but I woke 'im up. Sir – 'e's got fresh lash marks on 'is back.'

'Thank you, Clark,' said Peter. 'Drinks, please. Did Captain Dettner have anything to eat?'

' 'E 'ad a cup of tea and a sarni, sir.' The P.O. steward poured out gin and bitters for the Commander and whisky for his Captain. 'Made me cross, sir, to think them Indians would do a thing like that.' He went out.

'It makes me cross too, Bunny,' said Peter. 'I think I'll put in the report that the prisoner was assaulted while in the hands of the Indian police.'

The guest cabin opened off his cabin flat where the Marine sentry stood guard over the ship's keys. Peter went there after he had had his drink. Dettner was still asleep, sprawled on his face, naked under the sheet that only part covered his thin body. Peter took in the brutal weals on the fair skin: he must have had a round dozen, Peter reckoned. He noted the chafed wrist of the hand flung up by the pillow and, with some surprise, that the hand was calloused and salt-scarred.

Peter stood in silent contemplation for a moment. Then he looked about. The cabin was quite spacious with a table where meals could be served and a couple of armchairs. P.O. Clark had evidently done a little unpacking and he had placed a picture of *Prinz Ludwig* on the desk top. The gold-leafed cap was on the table and Peter peered at the badge but it meant nothing to him.

A sigh from the bunk made him look round. Dettner was stirring uneasily and he muttered a few words. Peter's German was fairly rudimentary but he thought he caught, 'So many – oh, God, not so many.' He was not surprised: most sea-going naval officers that he knew had their private nightmares in greater or lesser degree. He had his own, at times.

He went out, deciding to ask the Surgeon-Commander to give their prisoner a check-up. Back in his day cabin, Bunny was still browsing through a set of A.F.O.s, a fresh drink beside him. Peter helped himself to another.

'Still asleep,' he said to Bunny. 'What do you reckon?'

'I don't think he had any idea of what was in the crates,' the Commander said.

The next day was Sunday and Peter reduced speed so that Divisions could be held in comparative peace. The Padre conducted morning service.

Dettner had come on deck in fresh whites and Peter, remembering his clear singing voice at St Ordulph's drew him in beside him. But the clear voice was silent. They came to the 107th psalm and the words 'They are carried up to the heaven and down again to the deep: their souls melteth away because of the trouble.' Peter felt the man beside him shiver. He wondered what trouble was melting his soul. The blue eyes remained withdrawn and deadened. Was it the treatment, the humiliation he had received at the hands of the Indian police or something more distant, something from the war or in the aftermath of war?

Peter took Dettner and Bunny Hare to his day cabin after the service. He wanted a clear picture to put in his report.

'We all heard about your splendid signal to Admiralty, London,' he said when they had drinks. 'But what did you do after *Prinz Ludwig* had "proceeded Wilhelmshaven"?'

Dettner paused, looking down into his glass. Then he raised his head.

'They gave me a job on a harbour tug,' he said.

Bunny chuckled.

'*Kapitän zur See* – tugmaster!' he said.

'No – *Kapitän zur See* – deckhand.' Dettner gave the ghost of a laugh which almost broke. 'The tugmaster came later – ocean-going.'

Peter had a sudden appalling vision. We have surpassed the Treaty of Versailles, he thought. Have we humiliated them too far? Is this going to lead to more desire for revenge, yet another war – or have we got to keep them under for ever? Surely not: we must work with them, build them up again, restore some hope, some future for a man like this.

'How did you come to take on the *Neumark*?' he asked.

'I needed money for my family.'

'Your family – you're married?'

'No, I'm not married.' Dettner paused. 'But I have – I had – parents and my sister and her child. Her husband was still in Russia.'

Peter digested this household of responsibilities.

'You say you – had – parents?'

'My mother still lives. Your people were blowing up and sinking old ships. My father decided to go down – or up – with his.' He looked at Peter. 'The Commander who boarded *Prinz Ludwig*. He told me your sister was on board the *Curie* when I sank her.

The blue eyes were intense now, expecting or dreading – what?

'Yes,' said Peter, quietly. 'She was one of five Wrens. They took their chance with the rest of those crossing the Atlantic.'

'Yes – I see.' Dettner stood up. 'Thank you for the drink.'

He went out and Peter and Bunny exchanged appalled glances. They both had noted the desperate joke about his father's end – in circumstances which they could not imagine – the abrupt change of subject, and both suspected that he had got up and left them because he could no longer face them. Peter was reminded of the P.M.O.'s assessment.

'He's like a stretched wire. He's either got to loosen off or snap.'

Dettner went to his cabin. Peter's gentle response to his curt reference to the sinking of the *Curie* had knocked him off balance. He sat down in an armchair and his terrible grief could no longer be contained. He buried his face in his hands and gave way to silent, chest-wrenching tears of shame and despair.

Nobby Clark, opening the door with a cheerful remark on his lips about laying the table for lunch, only needed one glance before noiselessly withdrawing. He had seen it all before – but it was somehow reassuring to know that German officers went there too.

The Marine sentry, observing his stealthy retreat, said, 'What's the matter, Nobs? In a compromising situation?'

'Cryin' 'is guts out,' said Nobby, shortly. He went into the Captain's day cabin to lay the table there and remarked chattily 'I'll do Captain Dettner's in a minute. 'E seems a bit upset jus' now, sir.' He placed knife, fork and side-plate with finicky precision. ' 'Course one can on'y 'old on for so long. 'E'll feel better now 'e's given way.'

He added napkin, dessert spoon and fork, viewed the table with satisfaction and went out.

Captain and Commander eyed each other. Homespun wisdom? Bunny got up.

'I'll cut along to the Wardroom, sir,' he said and also went out.

P.O. Clark, re-entering the guest cabin with his tray of cutlery, found the occupant lying back rather warily in his chair, quite composed.

'Can I bring you a drink before lunch, sir?' he enquired, brightly. 'No chits, sir – you being a guest of His Majesty's Government, so to speak.'

Dettner smiled.

'In that case – some juice or mineral water, please.'

The ordered routine of a naval ship at sea was beginning to work a calming sense of security in him. The fear of incarceration and perhaps trial in an India torn by upheaval and rival factions had been great; the knowledge that he had been duped to take responsibility if the illicit cargo were discovered and the beating he had endured to make him admit that responsibility had done nothing for his already lowered self-esteem. The British Captain's probing in an endeavour to find a reason for his acceptance of a position as Master of a gun-running ship had tried him sorely. To evade it he had blurted out that remark about the Captain's sister. It was not something he could even make an apology for – one head amongst so many, if she had survived the initial bombardment.

The steward's entry with a tall glass on a tray interrupted his thoughts. He eased his back cautiously away from the chair and took the glass.

' 'As the doctor seen your back, sir?'

'Yes, he has, thank you,'

Dettner watched him go. Kind – oh, God, they were all so kind...

Moorhampton was at anchor the following day and Peter went ashore to report and to pick up further orders.

'You're going home, Peter,' said the S.O.(O). 'And taking your prisoner with you. Admiral Chalmers wants him safe. Apparently there are all sorts of rackets going on in some of these occupied ports – not to our credit. One is supplying out of work seamen for these dicey voyages. You can tell Dettner that, if you want to, though I don't doubt he has realised he was duped. But – don't tell him this: some people want him on the War Crimes list for the S.S. *Curie* business.'

'Oh, but surely,' said Peter, startled 'It's not as though it was a civilian liner. She was a troopship.'

'Yes. But why did he leave them? So many of them.'

Peter was reminded of the broken whisper: 'So many, oh, God, not so many.' Was that why, he wondered.

9

The voyage home was uneventful and *Moorhampton* was at last secured again alongside the jetty at her home port. The weeks at sea without alarms or the fear of submarines or surface or air attack had done them all good. The ship was going into dock for refitting and repainting, the ship's company on leave and to fresh posting.

The first ecstatic greetings of homecoming were over and the first leave-takers had departed when the khaki-painted staff car arrived at the dockside. Peter and Dettner stood on the quarterdeck and watched the occupants disembark – an Army driver, a sergeant with a rifle, a smartly-uniformed captain with a holstered pistol strapped to his belt. The first two stayed by the car while the Captain climbed the brow and saluted.

'Good day to you, Captain,' said Peter.

'Captain Jones, Sir,' he said with the suspicion of a Welsh lilt and turned bright humorous eyes on them both.

'This is Captain Dettner,' said Peter, gravely.

'Am I such a desperate character, Captain Jones?' said Dettner, looking at the holster and at the armed sergeant below.

'I hope not, sir,' said Jones, cheerfully. 'But an important one. Shall we go? North London to start with.'

Peter saw a steward hand over Dettner's suitcase to the driver who stowed it in the boot. He turned and held out his hand.

'Goodbye, Captain Dettner,' he said. 'I understand we shall be meeting again in London.'

'Goodbye. And thank you.'

Dettner saluted him and preceded his escort down the brow.

Bunny came down from the bridge and joined Peter. They watched the car swing round and head for the dockyard gates.

'War crimes!' said Peter, disgustedly and went below.

He went home to Greystone, a couple of days later. John, his son, was ten years old now and enjoying the long summer holiday from school. Admiral Sillifant, older and not so active as he wanted to be but recovered from his Atlantic immersions in his soft native air, was obviously impatient to hear about the Far East commission but contained himself while Peter and Kate strolled in the garden.

Peter gratified him the next morning and told him about Ceylon and about Hong Kong and Singapore, all places he had been familiar with. But said nothing about the trip to Calcutta and the prisoner he had brought back to England. Then he walked his father down to the local in the little village and re-acquainted himself with village life. He also re-acquainted himself with Dartmoor, walking there with his son and sorry that he and Kate could not ride there now as the horses had gone – Kate had no time to look after them properly. She had an elderly live-in housekeeper who, in time-honoured country fashion had been Morwenna's nurse, and a woman from the village came in two mornings a week to hoover and polish. The fact that 'Nan' lived in gave her a little more freedom as it meant that she did not have to leave either the old Admiral or his grandson alone in the house if she had to go out.

Peter had been at home for a week when Admiral Chalmers telephoned him and asked him to go to the Admiralty next day. He was to be there at eleven so he got up at six on a beautiful fresh morning already giving a promise of Autumn, got himself breakfast and set off on a quiet drive to London. He had not been there for some years and was disturbed that so much still lay in ruins.

Rear-Admiral Chalmers was alone at the desk in his office, a little greyer than when he had sent Peter and HMS *Curre* off to Seahaven but in much the same state of shabbiness so far as the office was concerned.

'Come in, Peter, nice to see you again. They're bringing Dettner over shortly.'

'From where, sir?'

Chalmers looked harassed.

'Well – it was a P.o.W. reception place. Still got a few awkward cusses who haven't been repatriated yet. But I don't want to keep him there – it's getting to him. I've interviewed him once. He's given us some useful information and we should be able to break up some of these nice little rackets.' He waved Peter to a chair. 'Peter – what in hell would you feel if your ship was taken from you and you were "directed" to some menial job by a little squirt of a W.O.?'

Peter shrugged. He had already tried to work that one out.

'I don't know, sir. But I do wonder what sort of resentment we're piling up. We left them some ships last time. This time we had to "abolish entirely and completely" I think the wording was.'

'The Potsdam Agreement.' Chalmers nodded. 'That's two years ago, now. Thing is – they won't give me a decision on the war crimes issue for about another month. If I keep him locked up for that time he'll go spare. He's already wilting.' The telephone rang and he snatched it up. 'Yes? All right, bring him up.' He put down the receiver.

'Give him to me,' said Peter.

'What?'

'Give him into my custody. I'll take him to Dartmoor.'

Chalmers stared at him for a moment. Then the door opened and the cheerful Welsh Captain came in, cap under arm.

'Ah, Captain Jones, thank you,' said Chalmers. 'Captain Dettner will not be going back with you. I'll give you a receipt for him. Have his things sent over here at once, will you?'

'Yes, sir.'

Peter stood up and held out his hand. Dettner looked tired and drawn but he smiled as he took the hand. He wore his stripped blue reefer with the plain gold rings and held his cap with the alien badge. Chalmers waved them both to chairs and rang for coffee.

'What badge is that?' he asked.

'A Danish line. We have no merchant marine now.'

'You knew the owner of the line? Which was why you were happy to take the job?'

'My father knew Nilssen. I thought "Admiral Slater" and "Commander Patel" were guarantee enough.'

'Patel,' grumbled Chalmers. 'Common as Smith.' He paused

while they were given coffee. Then he went on, abruptly. 'I'd like you to tell me about the assault on you in Calcutta.'

'To what end? You will be out of India, soon. What satisfaction can you expect?'

'The police there are retaining some of their British officers. They may tell us.'

'But it was a British officer.'

'What rank?'

'A – a Major.'

'Were you alone with him?'

'At first, yes.'

Chalmers eyed him, drank his coffee thoughtfully and got up to put the cup on a side table.

'Captain Dettner, did he molest you sexually?'

He swung round to see what effect the question had. But Dettner met his eyes, calmly.

'No. He intended to.'

Chalmers came back to his desk and sat down.

'He intended to,' he repeated. 'You were, presumably, secured in some way.'

'My hands were tied to the wall. They had only taken my shirt. He came to – strip me so I kicked him. The lieutenant thought he was calling for them. He came in with the Indians. Then they beat me. A whip, a cane, I don't know. Two strokes and a question. Two more and the same question. Ten or twelve, I think.'

'You don't seem unduly concerned,' said Chalmers, after a pause.

'I went to sea when I was twelve,' said Dettner. 'I was raped, I was beaten as a boy. One lives with it.'

They looked at him. He got up and put his cup beside Chalmers's and came back, a wry smile on his lips.

'Have I shocked the British Navy?' he asked. 'Does nothing like that happen in your ships? All your midshipmen are innocent and unsullied?'

'Well – they certainly don't get flogged – now,' said Chalmers, disconcerted. The ringing of the telephone saved him and he grasped it. 'Yes, sir. He is here now, sir. Quite convenient.' He looked at Peter. 'Admiral Everett,' he said and chuckled.

The door opened almost at once and the white-haired Admiral strolled in, bright eyes almost invisible in wrinkles of skin. The other three stood up.

'Won't interrupt you for long, Chalmers,' he said and held out his hand to Dettner. 'I had to meet the originator of that bloody impertinent signal.'

Dettner smiled.

'I hope I may be remembered only for that,' he said.

'Yes, well.' The Admiral laid his other hand upon the one he clasped. 'Fortunes of war, eh?'

He nodded to Peter and Chalmers and strolled out again. They sat down again. Peter could only think of the unemotional voice describing the assault. There was little doubt where he had kicked. Peter could imagine the savage backward kick and the satisfaction when it connected. The thought of the boy, the child, only two years older than his own son, raped and beaten, sickened him.

'Well, for the moment, I think that's all,' said Chalmers. 'See you both in about a month. I'll let you know, Peter. And thank you.' They shook hands.

'Am I to go with Captain Sillifant?' asked Dettner.

'Yes.' Chalmers chuckled. 'Used to be French and American prisoners in Dartmoor, I believe.'

'I have your parole?' said Peter.

'Yes.'

The man sounded a bit apprehensive but Peter did not allay his fears until they were in the car and heading out of London.

'I'm taking you to Devon,' he said, then.

'To Devon? Is Dartmoor still the same?'

'Oh, yes. Unchanged.'

'But – the prison? Am I still a gun-runner?'

'No. They have absolved you of complicity in that. You're not going to the prison. They don't take that sort of prisoner now. You're on parole, in my custody and coming to my home.'

Dettner was silent for a long time and then he said 'No,' flatly.

Peter drove on, considering. They were in countryside now and he looked at the clock on the dashboard. At the next reasonable-looking pub he swung the car into the park and turned off the ignition.

'No?' he said. 'You won't come to my home?'

'Your wife? Your father?' said Dettner, uncertainly.

'I'm just going to ring Kate, now,' said Peter, cheerfully. 'Then we'll have some lunch.'

'But you cannot —.'

'Oh, I'll get a subsistence allowance for you, if that's bothering you,' said Peter. 'Come on.'

Being that much nearer London, the fare was neither so good nor so plentiful as Peter's local served but they ate adequately and drank not very good beer. In the car again, Peter glanced at his passenger.

'Kate was very pleased,' he said, gently.

He knew the man was thinking of the missing member of the family — but that, also, he hoped to exorcise.

10

Kate and John met them at the door. It was bathed in sunshine again but there was only Kate and the toddler was a well-grown boy in grey shorts and a check shirt.

'I am so glad you are coming to stay with us,' said Kate, putting out her hand. 'You look as if you could do with some Dartmoor air. But I cannot go on calling you Captain Dettner. May I call you Hans?'

He touched her hand with his lips.

'Please – if you will," he said.

'Good. And I'm Kate. And you know Peter.'

'And I'm John, sir,' said John, firmly stating his position. He took up the well-worn suitcase that Peter had unloaded from the car and hefted it indoors.

Dettner looked concerned as it was obviously too heavy for the boy but Peter smiled and said, 'Let him be. Tea's in the garden. Come through.'

The Admiral was waiting for them, tea was laid, insects hummed in the trees, the occasional sound of moorland sheep came to them, an aeroplane passed far overhead; the gentle family conversation flowed around him and Dettner felt the tension slowly draining from him. His eyes rested on a distant view of the tors and he did not see the glance exchanged between Kate and Peter.

But it got cool quickly now and the Admiral gathered up his newspapers and turned to go indoors.

'An early-ish supper, I think, Kate,' he suggested as he went.

'We don't "dine" nowadays,' said Peter. 'Stay as you are. From tomorrow, as casual as you can manage.'

In the bedroom that John took him to, Dettner found the window also had a view of the moor. He wondered if it had been the sister's room, though it showed no signs of feminine occupation. He took Peter at his word and remained in uniform. He was too tired and dazed to change into anything else.

Kate took morning tea to her father-in-law. She also took a cup to the guest-room, tapped on the door and went in. The clear, cold morning light came in through the window and she stood silent for a moment. Then she went down to the kitchen where Peter was making toast.

'He's sleeping as if he never wanted to wake again,' she said.

Peter did not need to ask who. He had told her only a little of what he had learned but he knew her ready sympathy was touched.

But the Admiral, later, said, 'No – don't treat him with kid gloves. He's used to living hard. You'll break him down if you're too gentle. And don't stop John from asking what he likes. Children often find the best way.'

Hans Dettner awoke about eleven o'clock, disturbed at last by the sixth sense that tells a C.O. that he is wanted. He opened his eyes to see John looking down at him. He was instantly alert and his first realisation was that the day was well advanced, the second that the boy held a steaming mug. He glanced at the watch strapped to his wrist and his third realisation was that he had enjoyed 12 hours of undisturbed sleep for the first time in years. He pushed himself up on one elbow.

'Good morning,' he said. 'Is that coffee?'

The boy was staring now and his fourth realisation was that in pushing aside the bedclothes he had revealed the puckered scarring on chest and arm from the wounds that had put him in hospital before he had joined *Admiral Scheer*.

John held out the mug.

'What are those scars?' he asked.

'It was shrapnel – but only superficial.'

The boy was frowning as if puzzled and finding the answer inadequate.

'I'll run you a bath,' he said, hurriedly and went out, leaving Dettner almost as puzzled as the boy had looked.

John went downstairs and hovered by his father until he got his attention.

'Daddy,' he said, 'Captain Dettner has got a lot of scars up here.' He touched his chest and upper arm. 'I asked what they were and he said "it was shrapnel but only superficial". What did he mean?'

'He meant he was wounded by shell splinters but not seriously. Why, John? What worries you?'

'I knew people got wounded in war,' said John. 'I thought they got all better. I didn't know it stayed like that. Have you got any, Daddy?'

'Just some little ones.' Peter wondered how to explain to the child. 'They are better, John. It is just that the skin doesn't always get smooth again.'

Dettner, having taken the bath that John had run for him and put on some casual clothes in the form of khaki drill slacks and a white shirt without shoulder badges, came downstairs. He brought the mug with him and Peter took it from him with a smile.

'I think you needed that sleep,' he said. 'Breakfast?'

'No. No, thank you. Some more coffee?'

'Yes. We're just going to have some in the garden. Go out and talk to my father, will you?'

However, the Admiral had his newspapers. He looked up and Dettner, with a stirring of amusement, felt he might well be a junior officer joining his first ship.

'Ah, there you are,' said the Admiral. 'Had a good sleep? Sit down.'

John came and sat near him. He had a length of string and was rather half-heartedly playing cat's cradle.

'Can you tie knots, sir?' he asked. 'I'm trying to learn some.' He took another length of string from his pocket and hopefully held them out.

'What do you want the knot for?' asked Dettner.

'What do you mean?'

'Knots – bends and hitches – have a purpose. I don't know the English names but this one,' Dettner secured the two pieces, '– is to join two ropes –'

'Reef knot,' growled the Admiral.

'This to put a loop on a rope's end.'

'Bowline,' said the Admiral, putting down his paper.

'This temporarily to make the rope shorter.'

'Sheepshank,' said the Admiral, triumphantly. 'My God, it's a long time since I've done any of those!'

'Reef knot, bowline and sheepshank. Thank you, sir,' said Dettner. 'Now, you tie them, John.'

Both men were watching and guiding the boy twisting his pieces of string when Peter and Kate came out with fresh coffee and biscuits. John, having successfully accomplished the tying of all three, looked up at Dettner, thanked him politely and went on with the devastating frankness of childhood.

'They showed us some pictures of those camps at school, last term, you know, like Belsen. Is it true the Nazis burnt Jews in ovens?'

'John,' said Kate, 'I don't think this is the time—'

Dettner checked her.

'Yes, I understand so,' he said.

John essayed another bowline.

'Were you a Nazi, sir?'

'No. We weren't all Nazis but I suppose we were all guilty.'

'Why?'

'For allowing it to happen.'

John looked him straight in the face.

'Could you have stopped them?'

Dettner, trapped, looked for help from Peter who put up a hand to conceal the smile on his lips.

'No,' said ex-*Kapitän zur See* Dettner, taking the bull by the horns. 'By then we could not have stopped them. The mistake was in letting them come to power in the first place.'

John considered this then nodded. He came round to the man's side and gave him the piece of string.

'I can't quite get the sheepshank,' he said. 'Show me, please.' He watched carefully as the thin fingers manipulated the string slowly so that he could see each move and then took it to try again. 'What do you call it in German, sir?'

The Admiral was immersed in his paper again and Peter and Kate were happy to relax in the August sunshine, not taking a lot of notice of their son, satisfied that his victim could handle matters.

Then Kate got up to go to prepare lunch with Nan, and the Admiral put down his paper.

'I think a walk down to the pub would do us good,' he announced. 'Are you game, Dettner?'

'Game? Yes, sir.'

'Can I come?' cried John. 'I can sit outside.'

They let him come and he skipped along ahead of them, making a little song of the German words he had learned for his bends and hitches. They all sat outside in the sunlight.

That first morning set the tone of the next couple of weeks, except that Dettner did not oversleep again. The boy seemed fascinated by the visitor and begged to learn some German – it would be such an advantage when he went to his 'big school' next year, he declared. The man was quite happy to 'sing for his supper' if it relieved Kate from having to keep John occupied, particularly when the second week brought rainclouds and moorland walks became less attractive. The Admiral had not sufficient patience to entertain a ten-year-old for too long, Peter was often busy with papers that came down from Admiralty – he had admitted to Dettner that he was, reluctantly, on the 'dry' list for the time being and would be joining Rear Admiral Chalmers's staff at the end of his leave, though he hoped he would be given a sea-going command again at some future time.

Kate noticed that Dettner never stayed alone with the boy. If John wanted to walk then Peter went, too. If they were in the garden, the Admiral was in his garden chair. If John wanted to have his 'German lesson' in the sitting room, it was when Kate and Nan were nearby in the kitchen. Peter had not, in fact, told Kate but Dettner was well aware that an abused child is often suspected of becoming an abusing man. He knew, himself, that he had no such tendencies but he wanted nothing to spoil the pleasure of those days. What had seemed, when Chalmers had said 'about a month', an eternity to be foisted on to comparative strangers, now seemed to be only too short a time; the options of a trial for war crimes or a return to the silent and deserted yard at Ulsdorf filled him with dread. So he made sure that no possible shadow of suspicion could fall on the friendship that the boy offered to him.

11

Towards the end of the third week at Greystone, Peter took his 'prisoner' to Plymouth. Jasper Hare had got his fourth ring at the end of June and his ship was in port for a few days. They both were in 'civvies' and Peter thought again 'Savile Row' when he saw Dettner's grey suit. He wondered when the man had last been to London but the classic cut and impeccable tailoring did not date. He noted the black tie and remembered that Chalmers had forwarded a letter from Ulsdorf.

'Is it just a naval tie?' he asked as they drove across the moor. 'Or does the black have some significance?'

'My sister wrote to say that our mother died last month,' said Dettner rather dismissively.

'I am sorry. Why didn't she tell you sooner?'

'The letter has been some time in coming. Also —' He paused as if unsure whether or not to confide in Peter. 'We were — distant since my father's death.'

He had told Peter and Bunny the fact, now he outlined the circumstances. For just one tiny instant as he spoke of Albrecht on the bridge of the sole remnant of his fleet before it erupted in the explosions, Peter recognized the desperate pain behind the words.

'You were fond of your father?' was all he could find to say.

'They were my parents.'

In those four bleak words Peter recognized the sense of betrayal: by the father for what he had allowed to happen to his son; by the mother for letting him be party to his father's death.

He said no more.

Captain Hare was delighted to welcome them aboard his ship.

Peter had telephoned him beforehand, of course, and they lunched aboard in his day cabin and reminisced, mainly about Seahaven in 1938 and about the voyage back from Ceylon during which they celebrated his promotion.

When they got back to Greystone, Peter went to find Kate and John chased up the stairs to find his present hero. He found the bedroom door open and the one he sought washing his hands in the adjoining bathroom.

'What was the ship like?' he demanded. 'I wish I could have come. I like Captain Hare, don't you?'

'Yes, I do. The ship was like your father's last ship.'

'What was your last ship like?'

'Oh – a-a cargo ship.'

Dettner came into the bedroom and the boy laughed.

'Your last war ship, I mean.'

Dettner put his brushes down on the chest of drawers. He feared the outcome of this.

'Also like your father's – a cruiser.'

John perched himself on the bed. His next question was inevitable.

'What was it called?'

'Come – we must go downstairs.' The door was still open.

'Have you got a picture? What was its name?'

The picture was still in his case. He could not take it out in Morwenna's home.

'She was *Prinz Ludwig*,' he said.

John regarded him, gravely.

'That was the one that sank Aunt Morwenna's ship,' he accused. 'They said you left them all to drown.'

'John,' said Peter, in the doorway. 'Go down to Mummy.'

'No, Daddy. I want to hear.'

John bounced up and Peter put a hand on his shoulder – and waited.

'Yes,' said Dettner. 'I left them all to drown. I think, if Morwenna was in the Signals office, which would be abaft the bridge, she would have died in our first broadside which shattered it. The W/T office was not hit then and they got off their position and that they were under attack, before we destroyed them. I did not know how near were any ships. I had nearly a thousand men on board and there were as many, if not more, in the water. It was war.'

'Yes,' said Peter. 'It was war. Do you understand, John, why it must not happen again? Like the skin that won't get smooth, it leaves scars on the mind and in the soul. Can you understand?'

'Yes. I'm sorry.'

John went forward and lifted up his face for a forgiving kiss. Peter watched. The man who had known no boyhood and the boy just reaching out to manhood. Dettner bent and kissed the boy's forehead.

'Now, go down and ask Mummy if tea's ready,' said Peter.

John went out and they heard him go down the stairs.

'I would not have spoken so if you had not been here,' Dettner said.

'I wanted you to speak and I am glad he heard,' said Peter.

'Those you have to leave,' Dettner unconsciously echoed the Reservist, 'you do not forget them.'

'It is over, it is done,' said Peter. 'You must forgive yourself. We don't blame you.' But will the war crimes people, he wondered. 'Come down to tea,' he said.

Later that night, as they got ready for bed, Peter said, 'You haven't seen a lot of John these holidays.'

'No.' Kate smiled. 'But it has given me more time with you. I have John each evening and weekends – until he starts his "big school". He likes Hans. He says he has "truthful eyes".'

'You didn't mind that I brought him to stay here?'

'No, I told you.' She laughed. 'He even satisfies Nan's criteria – clean, tidy and polite! What's the matter, Peter?'

He sat down on the bed and she became serious.

'Time's nearly up,' he said. 'I think we shall be called back to London soon and God knows what then. As he said, they weren't all Nazis. We must give them back ships – a navy. You can't have a whole, inert, undefended mass lying in the middle of Europe. Take Dettner – Hans. The commander of a ship like *Prinz Ludwig*. So what did we reduce him to? Deckhand on a harbour tug – in order to get rations to support his family. Are they going to live with that, as a nation? Are they going to come back again to try to conquer Europe?'

'But you want to give them ships – to arm them again?'

'Yes. You can't strip them of everything, their honour, their pride – and expect them to be friends! Put me in Dettner's place. One swipe – no ship, no rank, no money, nothing.'

'But they lost – if they had won, they would do the same to us – or worse.'

'I know.' Peter got up and stripped off his shirt. 'So what do wars achieve? We either have to win their cooperation, to help them to rebuild – or else stamp them out of existence. Hell – I'm no politician. It all seems so futile when you try to see both sides of it.' He pondered. He had tried to express his muddled thoughts and had made a greater muddle. 'Kate, keep John here tomorrow. I'm taking Dettner to the moor.'

In the morning, after breakfast, Peter had a telephone call. He replaced the receiver thoughtfully and went back into the morning room where the Admiral and Dettner were still sitting talking while Kate and John listened and Nan cleared the dishes. The Admiral could be quite a raconteur without rambling in his story and he illustrated a point with an anecdote that made them all laugh. Then Dettner saw Peter and he got up still smiling.

'You want me?'

'Yes,' said Peter. 'Are you game for the top of Grey Tor?'

'Yes,' said Dettner, laughing again at the use of the word. 'I am game.'

'Can I come?' cried John.

Kate got up.

'Not today, poppet,' she said. 'It's school next week. We must go into town and get some things for you.'

'Oh, Mummy! Daddy, can't I come?'

'Not today, son.' Peter saw the keen, blue eyes glance from him to Kate and thought, he knows there's something in the wind. Aloud he said, 'Put on a sweater – it'll be breezy on the top. See you outside in ten minutes.' Then he caught Kate in the kitchen alone. 'London, tomorrow,' he said. 'I'll take the car to the moor and fill up on the way back.'

He was waiting in the car when Dettner came out of the house and crossed the gravel with his rather quick-striding walk.

He got into the passenger seat and said, 'Chalmers?'

'Yes.'

Peter drove off across the moor and to the gate that led to the stream at the foot of Grey Tor. They got out of the car and crossed the narrow bridge and Dettner paused to look up the 800 and something feet above sea level, the long slope dotted with sheep and ponies and carpeted in coarse turf and gorse and ling.

'I am not so fit as nine years ago,' he said.

'Nor am I,' said Peter. 'Let's see if we can make it.'

They made the top together, drawing deep, gasping breaths and sat down on the coarse grass in the shelter of the granite outcrop. It was the first day of September and the wind was keen but the sun shone and the sky was blue and almost cloudless. Far below, some riders were cantering through the russet bracken. For a long while they sat and looked at the ever-changing scene, until their chests had stopped heaving and their breathing was quiet again.

'When the war started,' Dettner said, slowly, 'this was where I wanted to be, the only place, it seemed, where I might find comfort. At sea, I think only the U-boat men had any thought of victory – and over thirty thousand of them died.'

'You –' said Peter, confounded 'went to war expecting defeat?'

The ex-*Kapitän zur See* did not reply at once.

Then, slowly, 'You do not understand the respect and admiration we had for the Royal Navy. When we went to sea we felt we were trespassing on Royal Navy preserves. We based everything on you. We studied Nelson's tactics at the Academy. How could we beat our masters? So, we did not seek battle. There was no Skagerrak – what you call Jutland. Hitler did not want war with England.'

'There was the Battle of the Plate.'

'Yes. But *Graf Spee* was a commerce raider and Langsdorff was ordered not to engage warships. As I was. We fought, off Norway, in the Mediterranean. In general, we were not to seek battle.'

'Did your men feel that defeat was inevitable?'

'No. Remember, we had a Political Officer on board. No subversive talk. And the broadcasts telling us of the victories on land, the thousands of tons of shipping sunk by the U-boats, the voyages of *Scheer*. But then you got her in dock and the U-boats, at the end, had a life expectancy of just over two weeks. All for one power-crazy fool.' He paused and sighed. 'I am talking,' he said, 'because I don't want to hear about Chalmers.'

'Chalmers,' said Peter, 'wants us there, tomorrow.'

'He said – nothing – about the war crimes?'

'No.'

Dettner was silent for a while, watching the changing sunlight and shadow on the side of the next tor as clouds passed over the sky.

'If they will lock me up,' he started, then stopped. The idea was evidently too much to contemplate. He went on, hesitantly. 'They gave Dönitz ten years. For sending out his U-boat packs? And Räder life – for invading Norway. For the camps, the extermination yes – but for fighting a war?'

'I don't believe, myself, that action against a troopship will count as a war crime. I think, possibly, there have been some errors of judgement. I am concerned about the immediate situation when you returned home.'

'It was explained that all forces were disbanded, all ships decommissioned...'

'But – as a senior officer –' Peter hesitated, 'was it humiliating to be given the jobs you were given?'

'As a senior officer – I felt they could have made better use of us. But perhaps I was unlucky. Perhaps I went to the wrong authority – the humiliation was not in the work but in the way one was directed to it.'

'They could have made better use of you,' Peter agreed. 'At some ports I believe they took on Captains of Dockyards, say, in an advisory capacity.'

'But I was Captain of a cruiser ... I think she has gone to Holland.'

'Royal Netherlands Navy? Reparations?'

'Yes. Perhaps I should have scuttled her – and gone with her. What is left?' He looked across the moor. 'I have come up to the heaven. Do I go now down again to the deep?'

12

They did not have to leave as early as Peter had done on his previous trip, being due at Chalmers's office at twelve-thirty. Peter was in uniform; Dettner had refused to wear his and had put on his dark grey suit.

'But, damn it,' said Peter crossly, at breakfast, 'you're still a Master Mariner, aren't you?'

'In what?' retorted Dettner. 'If I am not *Kapitän zur See* in a non-existent navy, how can I be Captain in a non-existent Merchant Marine?'

The Admiral looked from one to the other. They were both on edge, he was aware.

'Calm down, gentlemen,' he said. 'I doubt if it matters a jot whether or not you wear uniform. You are quite likely to find Chalmers in civvies. I shan't come out to wave goodbye so I'd like to say now, Captain Dettner, that I have enjoyed having you here and talking with you. I hope you will be able to come and visit again sometime in the not too far distant future.'

'You are very kind, sir.'

Kate and John, however, did come out to wave goodbye.

Peter had put the car ready on the gravel sweep outside the door and John thrust out his hand and proudly said, '*Auf wiedersehen, Herr Kapitän.*'

Dettner shook his hand and turned to make his farewells and thanks to Kate. When she did not offer her hand he stepped back and made her a slight bow. But she laughed, put her hands on his shoulders and kissed him warmly on the cheek.

'Goodbye, Hans. Good luck. Let us hear from you.'

She kissed Peter and stood by the door with John as the car went off down the drive.

Chalmers was in uniform. He got up and shook hands.

'Sit down, both of you. I take it you didn't stop for the papers?' He indicated some newspapers on his desk. 'You are not being charged with leaving the *Curie* survivors to drown, Dettner. It was agreed that, since they got off a signal giving your position you had to leg it as fast as possible. Unfortunately, it seems to have been leaked and some of the more vociferous dailies don't like it. So I'm flying you back to Germany this afternoon.'

He tossed over a couple of the papers, late morning editions. Both had a three-quarter length photograph of Dettner on board *Prinz Ludwig*, with a line of laughing sailors as background. He was in full uniform with the swastika and eagle on his breast and on his cap. He was also laughing and looked supremely assured and arrogant. The headline on one said 'Not Guilty of War Crime?' The other said '1,500 men and women in the water and he leaves them to drown.'

Neither Peter nor Dettner looked further.

'I go back to Germany today?' said Dettner, without comment on the papers. 'To what?'

'If you are prepared to cooperate,' said Chalmers, slowly, 'to the U.O. dockyard. You will be given the assistance necessary to repair and reinstate it – not, as yet, as a shipping line but for repairs and maintenance.'

'I am not a shipbuilder – I know little of business methods.'

'Do you mean you won't be a shipbuilder – or you have no experience?'

Dettner digested the difference and smiled reluctantly.

'I will learn to repair ships if that is what is wanted,' he said.

'Good. You see, we badly need men like you, over there. The Russians are recruiting in East Germany, mainly into police units at present but it will come to military forces. It is likely that we shall allow you a merchant marine by next year and later, I foresee, the nucleus of a navy. Are you ready to go back and prepare for that?'

Dettner got up and went to the window. He stood staring out but saw nothing of the London scene below. A navy again? Probably only destroyers, minesweepers and patrol boats. But a navy.

Chalmers cut into his thoughts.

'You're still a young man, Dettner. Forty-two? Forty-five to fifty is about right for a *Konteradmiral*.'

Dettner turned round.

'For God's sake!' he said, laughing 'What carrots are you dangling? I will go back. I will cooperate – as I did to bring *Prinz Ludwig* home for you!'

Chalmers chuckled and chalked one up in the air with his finger.

'Good!' That's fine,' he said. 'You will report to the Engineer Captain at RN H.Q. on arrival. And, Peter, you report to me here on Monday morning. Now, let's go and have some lunch.'

Peter drove home in a happier frame of mind than on the journey up. He took with him a couple of the London late editions so that the morning papers would not bring too much of a shock.

John, looking at the photographs, stabbed his finger on the medals.

'I know that's the Iron Cross,' he said. 'What's the one round his neck?'

'The Iron Cross he got for action off Norway,' said Peter. 'The one round his neck is the Knight's Cross which he received for sinking the *Curie*.'

John nodded.

'It was war,' he said and, folding the paper carefully, went off with it.

Hans Dettner, meanwhile, had been whisked off in a staff car to an RAF airfield and into a plane stripped of most of its internal fittings in order to carry supplies. It was getting cold and he extricated his badgeless bridge coat from his suitcase and put it on, thankfully, over the grey suit. They landed at the ex-*Luftwaffe* base at Hamburg and again a car, this time marked RN, swept him off.

It was well into the evening now but the big building where the car stopped still showed lights through most of the windows. The seaman driver directed him through the main door.

'First on your right, sir,' he said.

The first door on the right said 'Engineer Captain' plainly and unequivocally so he opened it and went in. A bright-eyed Leading Wren got up from her desk.

'Captain Dettner?' she said. 'Captain Harding's expecting you.' She led the way to an inner door and ushered him in.

Captain Harding was a big man with purple cloth between the gold rings on his sleeves. He held out his hand.

'Glad to see you,' he said. 'Have you eaten? Jane,' to the Leading Wren, 'get them to send up sandwiches and coffee, will you? Take off your coat and sit down, Dettner.'

The Leading Wren departed and Harding sat down behind his desk. He had an open file in front of him.

'Now, you left about the middle of May, didn't you? Quite an eventful trip, all in all. Well – there've been a number of changes here since then. Not least, I might say, to your – er – domestic arrangements.' He waited as the Wren opened the door to let in a white-jacketed steward carrying a tray which he put down on the desk. 'All right, thank you. That'll do. We'll help ourselves.'

He poured coffee and Dettner remained silent, wondering what changes had occurred. He was very hungry and accepted sandwiches and the hot coffee, gratefully.

'Your Mother – my condolences,' said Harding. 'It was a heart attack – you know? Well, your brother-in-law, Anton Wessel, and his wife and child were sent back to Oldenburg which is where his parents live and where he was born. He has work there so he can keep his family, though I believe you took responsibility when he was repatriated. Thing is, the house was empty, your house, so it was commandeered – er – it's the WRNS Quarters now.' He was encouraged by the amusement in his silent listener's blue eyes. 'So – your father kept a small apartment in the U.O. offices, bedroom, kitchen, so on, which has been put in order for you. A P.O. steward will come in daily to look after you –' He broke off as Dettner began to laugh.

'Chalmers must have been damned sure of me,' he said.

Harding grinned.

'Rear-Admiral Chalmers had no doubt that you would have a go,' he said.

'That I'd be game,' said Dettner, thoughtfully. 'Yes. What next?'

'More coffee? Good. Next – we'll put you up here tonight. It's too late to go out to Ulsdorf now. Tomorrow we'll go out and see the extent of the damage – get that seen to. Then we can start drafting in the necessary workers for repairs and maintenance. There'll be a fair amount of paperwork for you.'

'Just one thing. Shall I be safe – next door to the WRNS Quarters?'

Harding gave a crack of laughter.

'We shall get on, I think, Captain Dettner,' he said.

A RN car took them out to Ulsdorf in the morning. The German ex-petty officer steward was already there in his badgeless uniform and leapt to attention when he was introduced.

'Otto Mirsch, *Herr Kapitän*,' he said.

'Relax, Mirsch. I have no rank,' said Dettner.

'But you're still the boss,' said Mirsch with a grin.

'He'll not be very busy,' Dettner remarked to Harding as they went down the steps to the yard.

'No. He will come back to the mess after lunch and then come back in the evening. We have cars fetching Wren watchkeepers and bringing them back so he can fit in with them. Now then, what needs to be done here?'

The tour of the yard showed some bomb damage to be put right, vandalism and neglect to be remedied, rubbish and rubble to be cleared from the dry dock, rusting cranes to be checked and replaced if necessary.

'Right,' said Harding, 'I'll send out a work force and they can get cracking. And I'll send you some lists of artisans so you can start selecting the necessary gangs of dockyard maties.' He grinned. 'You'll find a lot of ex-navy artificers and so on. It shouldn't be too hard to select the useful ones. Goodbye. Send a message with Mirsch if you're in trouble.'

He went off in the car and Dettner looked for a moment across the lane to the house. Then he went back into the yard and up the steps to the office and the adjoining rooms which his father had arranged as a living apartment. The kitchen was as compact and neat as a ship's galley, the bedroom like a cabin with a bunk against the wall, a chest of drawers and wardrobe in which he found clothes which he had left at the house.

'Your things were brought over here when they cleared the

house for the Wrens,' said Mirsch. 'The other stuff was put in the attics which they're not using.'

'Very well,' said Dettner. 'See to my suitcase, will you please. Put the photograph of *Prinz Ludwig* in the office.'

The office had a couple of armchairs and would have to do as his 'day cabin' for, apart from a shower-room, that was the extent of his living quarters.

13

For a month Dettner was left alone to get on with his task. The workforce under a competent foreman did wonders in clearing the yard, rebuilding and replacing. The lists of artisans, welders, electricians, plumbers, arrived and Dettner sorted through them and started interviewing.

He was up when Mirsch arrived at half past seven with the car that picked up the Wren watchkeepers due on duty at 8 o'clock. Mirsch departed again in the car that brought the same Wrens back after their four-hour stint, returning late afternoon and leaving finally at eight o'clock in the evening. Dettner had found a shelfful of his father's books on the construction and maintenance of cargo vessels and suchlike literature and conscientiously tried to study at night. But he felt, insofar as power was concerned, they were somewhat out of date. The strong vibrations from *Prinz Ludwig*'s diesels were in his memory but not in the books.

Before and after midnight he could hear the departure and return of the watches, the sound of the car, the soft chatter of the girls, their called goodnights to the driver.

Then, in the early days of October, Mirsch brought an official envelope which proved to contain a brief memo from Captain Harding. 'My Inspector, Chief Officer Polruthan and assistant, Lieutenant (E) Blair, will visit the yard 0900 hours tomorrow to assess progress.'

He stood at the window and looked out into the yard. The bomb damage was no longer visible, the dry dock was cleared and the great watertight doors functioning again. Two serviceable cranes on tracks reared up on the dockside. It was all so familiar and so meaningless to him. His heart was at sea. He looked at the picture of the heavy cruiser, *Prinz Ludwig*, on the top of the filing cabinet and beside it, where he had stuck it on the wall in a fit of defiance, the picture of himself and the laughing crew members and the headline 'Not Guilty of War Crime?' taken from the London newspaper.

Perhaps it would be better when there were ships in the yard, perhaps sea trials. He recognised his ignorance about his father's business. He went out and down the steps to the yard, to find the foreman and warn him of the impending inspection.

The next morning promised fine weather but chilly. Mirsch brought him breakfast – the ex-P.O. was able to buy real coffee instead of the usual *ersatz* and white bread from the H.Q. canteen which was a bonus. Afterwards, when the work force arrived at eight o'clock, Dettner went out to make a preliminary inspection and hoped that Harding's inspector would be satisfied.

He was at his desk, checking through his handwritten lists of dockyard workers when Mirsch announced, 'The Inspecting Officers, sir.'

Both officers wore naval trousers and battle blouses with their rank badges on the shoulder straps. The lieutenant had purple cloth between the two gold stripes and curl and had tucked his cap under his arm. The other had three pale blue stripes and a diamond and wore her tricorne – a Chief Officer WRNS. She was a woman of some 30 years, of good height and slim enough to wear her uniform well. Dark hair, short cut, curled under the edge of the tricorne and dark eyes held a hint of laughter as if she were used to the surprise she caused.

Dettner gave them a brief bow, a mere bending and raising of his head, and came round his desk. She advanced, holding out her hand.

'Good morning, Captain Dettner. How do you do? I am Chief Officer Polruthan and this is Lieutenant Blair.' She spoke fluent German but as he shook hands with them both went on in English. 'I'm told you speak English well so perhaps we could use it.'

'I'm still learning German, sir,' explained Blair.

'Then, by all means. But what should I call you – Ma'am?'

'Not that, at any rate,' she said, laughing. 'What about Chief? I have a degree in marine engineering.'

'That is more than I have,' he said, ruefully.

'But you have other qualifications, Captain,' she said. 'Captain Harding said you were doubtful about your suitability for this but—' She looked him over and smiled. In anticipation of an extended tour of the yard he had put on uniform trousers tucked into short leather sea boots, a roll-neck sweater and leather jacket. 'I'm sure you'll cope,' she finished. 'Shall we go and have a look?'

It was a thorough inspection, through the refurbished workshops, down the ladder into the dry dock, along the quay to the cranes, to the basin to see how many berths were available and, after two hours, back up to the office.

Dettner opened the door to the passage off which his quarters were and offered them the opportunity to wash after the somewhat grimy tour. He went on down the passage to the galley at the end to wash himself at the sink there and told Mirsch to bring coffee.

When he got back to the office Chief Officer Polruthan was sitting in one of the armchairs; Blair was evidently taking his turn to wash.

'Can I see your lists of workers, Captain?' the self-styled Chief said. 'Did Captain Harding say how many you were to take on?'

'Initially, yes.' Dettner gave her the handwritten sheets. 'But it will depend on how much work there is.'

'Oh,' she said, abstractedly, perusing the list, 'the yard should be ready next week and there'll be two ships coming up-river at once. Captain Harding will be sending you details. I see you've chosen quite a number of ex-navy artificers and some of the foremen are older workers who were here with your father. A good mix, I'd say.'

'Thank you,' he said, meekly and she looked up and met his eyes.

'Don't mock me, Captain,' she said, gently. 'I do know what I am talking about. Oh! Coffee – bless you!' She took a mug from the tray that Mirsch offered her and Blair rejoined them; he had taken notes during the tour and pulled out his notebook to check over some of the points. When they had been satisfactorily dealt with, Chief Officer Polruthan stood up.

'We shall probably see you again next week,' she said and held out her hand.

Dettner took it.

'I do not mock you, Chief,' he said. 'I am too much in need of your support.'

He saw them to the car at the foot of the office steps and watched it pass out of the yard's tall double gates and into the lane. Then he climbed back up the steps to the office.

Arrived at Naval H.Q., Chief Officer Polruthan went to the Engineer Captain's office. The Leading Wren announced her immediately and Harding waved her to a seat. She pulled off her tricorne and sat down while he completed the letter he had in hand.

'Well, Jenna,' he said, putting down his pen, 'how is the gallant Captain doing? Out of his depth?'

'Anything but,' she said. 'A very alert and intelligent officer, I'd say. He has made out excellent lists of the proposed work force, all in categories, well selected to my mind. Perhaps we should run to a secretary for him! The yard should be ready for use by next week. He seems to know most of the contractors' men by name – all those we spoke to, anyway. I should say he had a good hold on his ships' companies when he was at sea.'

'You're impressed?'

'Yes. But –.'

'Ah! I thought there must be a "but".'

'Two things. It's not his job. He'll do it well but he's a seaman. Secondly,' she paused, frowning, 'he's stuck that picture up on the wall, the one in the papers a month or so ago, saying "Not Guilty of War Crime?" Can that still be rankling?'

'That I don't know.' Harding lit his pipe. 'I was never a deck officer but I have been topsides on occasion when we've had to abandon men in the water. It's usually a gut-tearing decision and only the Commanding Officer can make it. It's not a question of guilty or not guilty for Dettner. He knew he had to decide in favour of the safety of his ship and crew. But that doesn't make it any easier to leave people to drown.'

'Not even enemies? Troops who were coming to invade your country?'

'No. At sea – if you are a seaman – if there is a ship – or people – in distress, you go to their aid.'

'Although you've caused that distress in the first place?'

'Paradoxical, isn't it? It's like when you've knocked your opponent down you stand by ready to pick him up. You don't go and kick him in the teeth – not if you're civilised! Practically speaking, if he had had time to pick them up they would have outnumbered his crew.'

'A dangerous situation,' she conceded. 'I told him you'd be sending him details of the ships going up to the yard. I'll go up again when they've been there a day or two to see how the new workers are coping.'

She went unannounced and alone but for the German driver, wearing her battle-dress because, with the amount of obstructions and ladders in the dockyard and on board the ships, a skirted uniform would have been unthinkable. Mirsch, who met her at the office, told her that the Captain was on board the ship in dry dock. She wondered if this would mean a descent by ladder into the dock and an ascent also by ladder up the side of the vessel and was glad to see, when she reached it, that a gangway had been secured from the dockside to the ship's deck.

She found Dettner below decks immersed in technicalities with one of the foremen.

'Good morning,' she said, in German. 'Is there a difficulty?'

Both men turned.

'Good morning, Chief,' said Dettner. 'This is Joachim Hoche, the electrical foreman. Hoche, Chief Officer Polruthan is an Engineer Officer.'

The foreman bowed to her but did not speak.

'No difficulty,' said Dettner. 'You wish to see what is being done? Carry on Hoche.'

He took her on a tour of both ships, making the various departmental heads known to her and, again, making her impressed and just a little chastened. Then he took her to the office, called to Mirsch for coffee and produced the lists of defects for her and the work being undertaken to rectify them.

'I don't suppose you've been over to your house since it became a Wrennery,' she remarked as she handed back the papers.

'No,' he agreed.

'I shall be coming over one evening next week to give a talk,' she said.

'You do not live there?'

'No.' Apart from the Quarters Officer and staff they are all Wren Watchkeepers – coders, teleprinter operators, switchboard operators, telephonists, so on – and a lot of their categories will not be needed for much longer. So I have to talk to them about remustering and the types of openings both in the Service and outside. Would you like to come over? Captain Harding and Lieutenant Blair are coming to give me moral support so you won't be a lone wolf amongst lambs.'

'Yes, very well. Thank you.'

It would be interesting to see what had been done to the house since it had been commandeered.

'I'll send Tommy Blair to escort you,' she said, smiling.

'Thank you,' he repeated, gravely. 'My nerve would fail on the doorstep otherwise.'

She got up, laughing.

'I very much doubt that, Captain Dettner,' she said. 'Next Wednesday evening, then. Goodbye.'

14

The Wrennery struck warm, compared to the old days, when the Duty Quarters P.O. opened the door to Lieutenant Blair and his civilian-suited companion. They had installed central heating, Dettner noted, disposed of the big stoves favoured by Albrecht and Hanna and painted the walls cream and the doors in Wren blue. The effect was bright, fresh and quite a shock to the dispossessed owner of the house.

He and Blair were welcomed by the one-ring Quarters Officer and taken into what had been the big kitchen and now appeared to be the Wrens' dining hall. Tables had been pushed to the wall and chairs lined up to face a small table where Chief Officer Polruthan was laying out pamphlets on various career opportunities both in and out of the Navy. Two rows of chairs were already decorously occupied by young women of various sizes and ages in their blue uniforms with the pale blue badges of rank and category on their sleeves.

Dettner wondered not only what on earth had persuaded him to accept the Chief Officer's invitation but also why on earth Harding and Blair were attending. They took seats at the back of the room and the Third Officer stood up by the small table and told the assembled Wrens the purport of the talk, which they knew, and Captain Harding introduced the speaker and made the point, illustrated by her as a marine engineer, that many more career openings were available now to women than before the war. Dettner decided that Blair must be there in attendance on his seniors and Harding to add the weight of some top brass.

The Chief Officer made her points very well. She indicated to them the relevant pamphlets which they could pick up and read afterwards, extolled the virtues of choosing a satisfying and rewarding career rather than just being a typist or shop assistant, rounded off her talk in half an hour and asked for questions. There were none. Which left a hiatus. She smiled at them.

'Well – that leaves us with some time in hand,' she said. 'So I am going to ask Captain Dettner who, as you know, owns this house and the dockyard–' he raised his eyebrows as she said 'owns' and wondered what questions she had for him; then froze in horror as she went on, '– if he would kindly talk to us a little about the view from the other side.'

She sat down beside Harding who said 'Bitch' under his breath.

Dettner went forward slowly and stood to one side of the table, looking at the brightly expectant faces of some dozen and a half British girls, his mind totally blank. The view from the other side? It recalled scenes from long ago and he started quietly.

'When I had command of the destroyer *Seehaven* in 1938, we made a courtesy visit to Seahaven in Devon.'

He stressed slightly the difference in pronunciation between the two names and, drawing entirely on the vision in his mind, went on to describe the camaraderie that had developed between his ship and the British destroyer, the swimming and sailing sports enjoyed between the two crews; the necessity for loyalty, support for each other; the peace and quietude of the visit to Dartmoor. He did not speak of the war except as he finished.

'We made friends then. Some have survived the war and I have met them since. We are still friends.'

He was not prepared for the girls' applause, nor for Harding's warm handshake.

'Bravo.' said the Engineer Captain. 'Off the cuff – that was splendid.'

The Wrens had now rapidly rearranged the room, pulled out some tables and pushed aside the chairs. Stewards brought in plates of sandwiches and trays of coffee mugs which they offered to their guests before distributing them on tables for the other Wrens, now busily leafing through pamphlets, to help themselves.

Jenna Polruthan, aware that she deserved Harding's epithet, knew Seahaven, being on Cornwall's doorstep, as it were, though she came from a good deal further West. Pisky-ridden, she made bad worse.

'Quite the Commanding Officer,' she murmured. 'Ever ready to speak to the troops!'

Dettner was silent. Fortunately, Harding turned back to him.

'What do you find to do in your spare time – if any?' he asked.

Dettner shrugged.

'What one does at sea,' he said. 'Read, listen to the radio, take a walk round the deck.'

'H'm. You must come out to the Base, sometime.'

He went off to have a word with a group of Wrens looking at higher education leaflets.

Dettner found the Quarters Third Officer, thanked her for the hospitality and quietly withdrew. He felt he could consider himself as of equal rank to the Engineer Captain and need not wait for that officer to leave first. He crossed the lane and unlocked the inset door in the tall gates to the yard and went in. One of the nightwatchmen bade him goodnight and he went up to his quarters. He felt vaguely disturbed. He was not sure what he had tried to convey to the girls but they had seemed to appreciate it and their clapping had been spontaneous. The Chief Officer's waspish remark afterwards seemed out of character as had her challenge to him to speak. Yet what had made her ask him to go to a thing like that except to hear her address the Wrens? Which argued that she had sought to make some impression on him. Or was it just to offer him the opportunity of seeing something of what had happened to his old home?

At breakfast the next morning the solitary letter in the post was from Peter Sillifant. Since his bread-and-butter letter to Kate he had received one letter from Peter who now spent his week in London but got back to Greystone most weekends. He had replied to that but not immediately and now, after a lapse, was Peter's return letter. It hadn't a lot to say: the Admiral was well, Kate was well, John was doing well at school. Peter would possibly be visiting Kiel or Wilhelmshaven shortly. Hoped all was well. As Ever. Dettner put it in his desk drawer, sighed and turned to the latest stores indents from his three foremen.

A couple of weeks later, a bitter day in late October, he was standing on the quayside, watching the merchant vessel backing into the river under her own power, from the now-filled dry dock, a fussy little harbour tug waiting to assist, if necessary, in swinging her round to face down-river for her journey back to the sea. Above the signals from their sirens between the ship's skipper and the tugmaster, came the familiar heavy throbbing of turbines. Dettner swung round to stare down-river and could see the very familiar outline of a MGB coming upriver, its small white ensign fluttering from the gaff of its stumpy mast. The bridge officer, skilfully avoiding the busy tug, indicated that he wished to come alongside and Dettner waved him into the inner basin, to leave the channel in the river free for the merchant vessel. By the time the ship, tow rope secured, was on its way in the wake of the tug, the MGB had found itself a berth and Peter, his greatcoat collar turned up about his ears, was walking across towards the graving dock.

'Good God, Hans,' he called, 'I didn't realise the yard was this size!'

'Peter – it is good to see you. Come into the office – it's freezing.' He led the way across the docks, Peter looking about at the activity, at the other vessel moored to one of the jetties. 'Are you all right down there?'

'Yes, they're fine, for half an hour or so. Unfortunately, I can't stay longer.' He followed Dettner up the steps to the office and accepted coffee. Then he pulled a bottle of whisky from his coat pocket. 'Thought you might be a bit short of the "real stuff",' he said. 'How's it going?'

'It's going well – I think. I am paid, my men are paid, my stores are supplied. I don't know what sort of debts I am piling up.'

'I shouldn't worry,' said Peter. 'Obviously we're going to have to offer a great deal of financial aid. But you're hardly going to be put on your feet again just to be bankrupted by accumulated debts.'

'Is this what we fought a war for?'

'We all know what Hitler had in mind. Personally, I fought it to get rid of him and his ambitions. Not to beat you into subservience. But I would like to know who financed the man: who kitted out and paid his stormtroopers before he came to power.'

'I don't know. I had no interest – there was order, there was employment. Work for this yard, ships being built, even warships – there was pride again. We let it happen.'

Peter got up. He turned to the picture on the wall by the filing cabinet and tore it down.

'It is over,' he said. 'You have to work for the future. No guilt. I must go.'

They walked back across the yard to the basin. The MGB's Captain came up on deck as they approached.

'Bring your friend aboard, sir,' he called. 'We've time for a quick one before lunch.

'Totally illegal,' said Peter. 'Come on, Hans.'

There were just two wardroom officers there, the C.O., a lieutenant-commander and his Number One, a lieutenant. The sub. was manning the deck with a leading seaman. Both officers were concerned about the usual post-war axeing and doubtful about their futures. However, they managed to treat the matter fairly lightly and entertained their passenger and his guest cheerfully. Dettner had a drink with them, complimented them on their craft and regretted its likely decommissioning and went back on to the jetty to see them manoeuvre away and disappear down-river. He went back to the office and poured himself a measure of Peter's whisky. Britain must be drained after a world war such as this. For how long could she offer financial aid to her defeated enemies? For how long would they go on accepting? Until they prospered again and then turn to bite the hand that fed them? He found, to his dismay, he could not, in his heart, trust his own people. After Versailles they thought only of the humiliation it brought them. Now – with 'all armed forces to be completely and finally abolished' – would they let that rest? Not another war. The nuclear weaponry made that unlikely. Then how? What form would retaliation take? Trade war? He didn't know. As he had told Chalmers, he was not a businessman. He had no knowledge of financial and currency manipulations. The description of simple sailorman seemed apt. What had he cared while he learned to sail a ship, to master tactics, to fight a battle, to command men?

Mirsch came out of the galley, silently laid the table and placed the meal upon it. The watchkeepers' car was about to return and he to go with it.

15

Some of the men, mainly the older ones, working in the yard, lived in Ulsdorf; others were bussed in or came on bicycles. They were a good lot, ready to work and glad of the opportunity to do so. The visit of Peter and the MGB had only increased Dettner's heartache. It was stupid and futile, he knew. He could not be part of a navy that had been abolished. He looked at the photograph that Peter had torn down and put on the desk. How confident and assured he had been then. He crumpled it slowly and dropped it in the wastebin. A copy of the original was somewhere amongst his things. It had been sent to him by the newspaper which had published it after he had been awarded the Knight's Cross. Of little worth, now.

Work was continuing on the second ship sent to the yard and a third was due in the morning to replace the completed one. The WRNS marine engineer had not been to the yard for about a month now but would probably come to see the new job.

She did – in company with Captain Harding.

'I've had good reports of the yard,' he said. 'Thought I'd come out again now it's in action, so to speak.'

Jenna Polruthan had worn her regulation uniform to the Wrennery talk but was back in battledress today, as was Harding, which was as well since they not only toured the yard but also inspected the half-completed ship and thoroughly examined the new job. The sun was well over the yardarm when they went to the office to discuss what they had seen and to estimate completion dates and Dettner offered coffee or whisky. They both chose whisky.

'I say, where did you find that?' Harding exclaimed when he saw the bottle.

'Peter Sillifant brought it.'

'Captain Sillifant? Chalmers's Chief of Staff?'

'Yes. He was – one of the friends who survived.'

'I am very sorry,' said Jenna, 'if I caught you unawares that evening.'

'It was no matter.' Dettner contemplated the golden liquid in his glass. 'As you said, one is prepared to speak to the troops on all occasions.' He looked at Harding. 'It was interesting to see the changes in the house.'

'Yes. It was somewhat neglected, of course – wartime and so on – but it should be in good order when you get it back.' He tossed back the remainder of his drink and stood up. 'Well, come on, Jenna. We must go. I'm very pleased, Dettner. The yard's doing well.'

Having seen them go, with polite handshakes all round, Dettner climbed back up the steps and paused on the landing outside the door to look out over his domain. Well, it was not a ship but it was the nearest he was going to get to one for the foreseeable future. It was doing well: it was up to him to see that it continued to do so. He had his quarters, the day and sleeping cabins, the steward in the galley. If there were no throbbing diesels there were the familiar noises of the yard, the occasional sirens on the river. He must stop yearning like a child for the unobtainable toy. He went inside. There was not a lot left in the whisky bottle.

In belatedly accepting the position he was in and removing the barrier of his unconscious resentment at being forced back to the yard which he had hitherto rejected, he found imagination and interest stirring. He took out the plans of the new job and spread them on the chart table.

In the drawer of the table he had found his father's instruments – compass, dividers, protractor, parallel rulers – but, unlike Albrecht, he was no marine architect. Nor was he an engineer. He knew the difference between water-tube and fire-tube boilers and between turbines and the reciprocating engine which *Neumark* had used in the winches. *Prinz Ludwig*, of course, had internal combustion engines but, in any case, he had left all that to his Chief and Senior Engineer Officers. So he did as he had done in his ship and sent for the Chief Engineer.

The response was not as immediate as he was used to. It was the next morning, on going in to see the Engineer Captain and make her report on sundry matters she had been dealing with in Fremenshaven, that Jenna Polruthan was startled to hear that her attendance at Ulsdorf had been asked for – or demanded. Harding chuckled.

'Seems he's got a bit stuck on something he thought of for Job Three,' he explained. 'You'd better get out there and sort him out.'

Job Three was a 7,000-ton cargo vessel which had suffered an internal explosion and fire which had wrecked a great deal of the interior, including the engine room. Externally, the hull was undamaged and she was secured to one of the jetties. They had been over her the previous day with Captain Harding and agreed a reinstatement programme but in view of the almost complete stripping of the interior, Dettner had thought of a different reconstruction. Jenna found him in the burnt-out bowels of the ship in company with the engineering foreman.

She listened to the proposed plan. Some she thought would work, some she was doubtful about, some she vetoed. She was pleased to find that he did not reject her advice but was prepared to listen when she explained why this or that would not work and accept her decision.

'You've got the original plans of this ship?' she said. 'I think we should have a look at them.'

Dettner took her back to the office; the foreman and his gang continued to strip down the machinery. The plans were still on the table and they studied them together. Jenna drew in lightly with pencil the proposed redesign and pointed out why this was feasible and why that couldn't work. She was quiet and tactful because she knew that he was used to dealing with male officers of long experience and he strove to follow into realms of technology where he had never before ventured. And she knew that he saw her at that time only as an engineer officer and not as a woman.

At length, he called Mirsch for coffee.

'I know so little,' he confessed, sadly.

'You don't need to know it, Captain Dettner,' she said. 'You have experts to advise you. You coordinate their knowledge. You know how to deal with men and how to use what they tell you. In your ship you had your navigator, your gunnery officer, your signals and W/T officers – you couldn't possibly have known it all. But you used their knowledge.'

He stared at her, brows knit, willing to be convinced. She laughed and raised her mug in mock salute.

'I said you'd cope,' she reminded him. 'You are reconciled to this, now, aren't you? I can feel it. What happened?'

He smiled and waved her to an armchair, sinking into the other.

'One cannot go on crying for the moon,' he said.

'But if you were offered a ship, you'd be off like a shot?'

'No. If I were offered the chance to help rebuild the navy –'

'That is your first love. But now – just at this time – what would you like most?'

But he laughed at her.

'A bath, I think.'

'A bath! Why?'

'You can't dream in a shower.'

She considered him and continued the bantering.

'And what would you dream about?'

The vision of the sleek shape of a beautiful ship in sunlit waters.

'A blue sea under a blue sky,' he told her and got up to take her empty mug.

She rose, too.

'Splendid,' she said. 'I'll tell Captain Harding of the revised plans and get his go-ahead. I'll let you have his answer tomorrow. Goodbye.'

He saw her to her car and went back to Job Three.

Jenna went back to Captain Harding.

'He's very good,' she said, soberly. 'And he's learning fast.'

She, however, had a lesson to learn. The only daughter and second child of a wealthy Cornish family, her father had also been a marine engineer and she had spent most of her childhood 'messing about in boats' with him until, near the start of the war, he had been killed in an accident during sea trials. She had been at university and following that at Engineering College, entering the WRNS with a commission in 1942. She was fiercely independent and rarely went back to the family home which was now occupied by her mother and brother with his wife and three children.

That evening she was going 'slumming' with a like-minded

Commander RNVR who should have known better but wanted to see some low-life in the dock area. They both wore what they considered to be fairly scruffy civvies but had not fully realised the total poverty and deprivation in that area.

Hans Dettner had also decided on an evening out that night. Once Otto Mirsch had served his supper and departed, he felt the need to be among other humans, to visit, as it were, the mess decks – he had not the money to go to the better hotels where the more affluent citizens went, the officials and civic dignitaries, the officers of the Occupying Forces and their hangers-on. He walked to the port, the well-known journey he had made so often after his initial visit to C.W.O. Martin, now blessedly forgotten. The bar he occasionally patronised was one of the cleaner, less sleazy ones that served decent beer or schnapps, put on a small cabaret and had hostesses who did not pester.

He chose a secluded table, ordered beer and rejected the attentive girl. He had not come seeking sex and would not have done so in Fremenshaven anyway. A group of five men at a table across the room he recognised as U-boat ex-officers, not yet drunk but bidding fair to get that way. He did not immediately recognise nor take much note of the rather more smartly clothed man and woman who came in shortly after his own arrival.

An older man who had been one of Albrecht's shipmasters came to join him.

'I hear you're getting the yard going again, Hans,' he said. 'When will they let you have some ships, too? Remember me when the U. & O. are sailing again.'

They talked, as always, of old times until the ex-skipper drained his schnapps, jerked a head towards the ex-U-boatmen and got up.

'I go before they start to sing,' he said.

Dettner thought he was probably wise and was about to follow him when the owner of the bar came up and sat down at the table so as not to be too conspicuous. They had known each other since the boy Hans had been an apprentice in his father's ships. The U-boatmen were beginning to sing, a fairly innocuous ditty but aimed at the British navy.

'Can you persuade those two English officers to leave?' said the bar owner.

'English? Where, Rudi?'

Rudi nodded across the room towards Jenna and her companion who were beginning to look a shade uncomfortable.

'Bloody fools!' muttered Dettner. 'How did you know she was an officer?'

'I've seen her about the docks in uniform with a young lieutenant.'

'Yes. All right. Bring us some schnapps.'

Dettner got up and went across to the other table. The U-boatmen were getting into the swing of it.

Jenna, recognising him in his navy slacks and roll-neck sweater and the black leather jacket, was overwhelmed by a surge of feeling which she did not think was purely relief at the idea of succour from an increasingly awkward situation.

'Will you have a drink with me? I think it would be wise,' he said as Jenna's companion rose to his feet.

'You could be right. Please sit down,' said the Commander.

'This is Commander Howard, Captain Dettner,' said Jenna and the surprised Commander shook hands. 'Some of the natives don't seem friendly.'

'They were U-boat officers and are now unemployed,' Dettner said. 'I think it is a little too soon to expect them to welcome you.'

'We realise we've been foolhardy, sir,' said Howard. 'It gets a bit boring to stick to the wardroom and a bit expensive uptown.'

Rudi came up with a tray and three glasses which he put down before them. Dettner gave him a note, his last one.

'I don't drink schnapps,' said Jenna.

'You will drink schnapps, Chief, said Dettner, equably, 'And then we go.'

Howard glanced from one to the other but maintained silence. He copied Dettner in tossing back the liquid and after a moment Jenna followed suit.

As they crossed to the door, the five singers fell silent, leapt to their feet and stood rigidly to attention. Dettner nodded to them and thankfully got his two companions out into the street. There were no cabs so he walked with them until they were clear of the area.

'I must thank you for getting us out of a difficult situation,' said Howard.

'If I had seen you earlier I would have advised you to leave. You should be all right now. Goodnight.'

16

The shrilling telephone woke Dettner next morning. He rolled out of the bunk, pulled on a bathrobe and went into the office. It was six o'clock and cold.

'Dettner? Harding here. Can you take a rush job? I've got nowhere to put her here. Ran into some submerged wreckage and got a gash in her bottom.'

'Yes. What sized vessel?'

There was a short pause.

'She's a destroyer. So a bit of hush, eh? I'll send her up under a passage crew with a diving team. All right?'

She came up-river at half past seven, creeping along with the gash boarded on the inside and two compartments sealed off behind watertight doors. Dettner, standing on the dockside, directed them into the dry dock, the heavy gates being open to the river. While they were ponderously sliding shut, Dettner, with the aid of the two ex-P.O. nightwatchmen and the ship's seamen, got her moored fore and aft to both sides so that she was held in the centre of the dock. Then he hailed the Captain.

The destroyer's C.O., a lieutenant-commander RN, came to the wing of the bridge, shadowy in the pale November light.

'Do you want to use the divers first or shall I empty the dock?'

Dettner thought it would be a waste of time to send the divers down but that was up to the destroyer's Captain.

'No. Empty the dock,' was the short reply.

Fortunately, the workforce were now arriving and were immediately put on to preparing and positioning the shores to support the ship in an upright position as the water left her high and dry.

The C.O. and what officers had come up-river with the ship, disappeared, no doubt to breakfast. As his would now be ready and waiting, Dettner did so, too.

It would take a while to pump the dock dry so he went on with the detailed plans and costings for Job Three and was immersed in the drawings when Harding rang again.

'Look, Chief Officer Polruthan is coming out now,' he said. 'Send the officers back in her car and I'll send out the workers' bus for the crew and the divers. OK?'

Dettner put down the phone and looked out across the yard. The destroyer had winched a brow to the dockside and the C.O. and his Number One were coming ashore. He returned to the chart table.

Lieutenant-Commander Bowyer was not happy and Dettner did not blame him for he was probably facing an enquiry and court martial. He stalked into the office and frowned when he found only one of the three workers who had moored his ship earlier that morning.

'Are you the Director?' he asked, looking around the office. 'Or isn't he here yet? He noted the meticulous plans, the photograph on the filing cabinet. 'I want to ring for a car to go back to base. I'll leave my First Lieutenant here.'

'The Engineer Chief Officer is coming out now,' said Dettner. 'You are to go back in her car.'

'Her car?' said Bowyer, startled.

'Yes. It has just arrived.'

Dettner saw the staff car draw up at the foot of the steps and a moment later Jenna opened the door and came in. She looked at the three men, the angry C.O., the effacing Number One and the faintly amused Dettner.

'Good morning, Captain Dettner,' she said. 'I see the ship's in dry dock and almost ready for inspection. That's quick work. Commander Bowyer – how do you do?'

'How do you do, Ma'am,' he replied, formally. 'I understand we are to take your car.'

His eyes strayed to the photograph and back to Dettner.

'Yes,' Jenna said. 'It will come back for me. Report to Commander (Ops).'

When they had gone, she turned to Dettner.

'Why did you make me drink schnapps, last night?' she said.

'You had to be seen to drink with me and we did not have time for beer. You knew – it could have become dangerous.'

'Yes. But why? We were not being superior or triumphant or whatever.'

'Those men were used to being great heroes, to coming off patrol and being feted. Now they are nothing and have nothing.'

'But you lost! You went to war and you lost it. Are we expected to go on treating you as heroes?'

'No. Just as humans. Because we can be hurt and humiliated and will cry if we have no hope.'

'We did not always have reason to think of you as human,' she said and saw him accept that. 'Have you – cried?'

'Many times.' He looked out of the window to see if the foreman was signalling the draining of the dock. 'You don't know the fear – the desolation.'

'No,' she said. 'No. We have no conception of total defeat – of occupation of the country. I cannot begin to imagine it.'

'That,' he said, rather acidly, 'is very obvious. Sometimes I wonder if you do not see us as just another lot of niggers in another colony.'

'Oh, no!' she said, distressed. 'Oh, surely not!'

He saw the foreman's signal and pulled on his leather jacket.

'Come,' he said. 'The dock is drained. We will see what needs to be done.'

She went with him, her mind struggling with the picture he had put before her. She thought of the ex-navy personnel who worked in the docks and the base stores and offices in their uniforms stripped of all insignia, under the orders of petty officers who did not speak the language but expected to be understood. She thought of the Raj and the Indians so recently made independent. She thought of the African colonies and the way they had prospered under Colonial rule and she thought it couldn't be all that bad. But a proud, white nation in defeat, in subjugation? Was it any different? Wasn't it what they had done to the Czechs and the Poles?

They went across the yard and down the steps recessed in the dock wall. They were slimy and wet from the recently drained water and Jenna's shoe slipped. For an awful moment she thought she was going to go rolling to the bottom but Dettner caught her arm and jerked her upright again. They did not speak.

On the floor of the dock, the foreman shipwright and the destroyer's First Lieutenant were viewing the torn plates. She must have struck the wreck at some speed for the gash was extensive.

'We were on the way home to decommission,' said the First Lieutenant, moodily.

'And you were on watch, I suppose,' said Jenna, sympathetically.

She could hear Dettner and the foreman discussing in their own language size and number of plates and rivets required or in stock.

'How long, Captain?' she asked.

'If we can get the necessary stores by tomorrow – three days.'

'Give me a list of what you want and I'll have them sent out today,' she said.

The First Lieutenant looked from one to the other.

'A three-week job at home,' he said, blankly.

'Were you hoping for leave, Lieutenant?' Jenna teased him.

He grinned.

'The chaps were cursing at the idea of being stuck in barracks for three weeks,' he said. 'I expect everyone's writing home to say they'll be back just in time for Christmas!'

The foreman indicated the buckled and twisted metal.

'We get on with cutting this away, now?' he said.

'Yes, carry on. Come, Chief – we'll make out those lists before your car comes back.'

They went back to the office and Mirsch brought them coffee.

'I think we can take time for a break,' said Jenna and sat down in an armchair.

Dettner remained for a bit at the window, looking out.

'You're hankering after that destroyer,' she said. 'Do you really think we treat you like natives in a new colony?'

'Oh – Hitler admired your Colonial rule,' he said and came to sit down in the other chair. 'He thought to emulate your rule in India when he had colonised Russia. But it all turned backwards. And we had such envy of your Navy because of the stations they could go to – the Far East, South Africa, Australia. We – made courtesy visits to Ceylon. He smiled, wryly. 'To Seahaven.' He shrugged and pulled a clipboard towards him. 'It is finished.'

She watched him as he wrote out, clearly and precisely, the list of requirements for Job Four and thought with a strange anger 'What a bloody waste'. She heard the car enter the yard and pull up below.

'I'll get this duplicated,' she said, taking the list from him and standing up. He went down to the car with her and, as she was driven off, went back to the dry dock and the graceful, crippled ship.

Both Jobs Three and Four were in full swing throughout the day. The requirements he had listed came out on a blue-painted RN lorry during the afternoon and Dettner checked them in and signed the duplicated list. By six o'clock, when the work force left, he had had, apart from brief meal breaks, a very full twelve hours. This, at sea, would not have been unusual but tonight, by the time Mirsch departed, he was more than weary. The radio in the form of a classical concert, kept him company for an hour or so. A book helped to pass some more time, then he went and showered and turned in.

Strange turbaned figures from Hitler's favourite film *Lives of a Bengal Lancer* invaded his sleep and merged into the two turbaned policemen in Calcutta and the superior lieutenant with his swagger cane and his clipped orders to the Indians. Then the khaki drill-clad major with his heavy-lidded eyes and his precise tones. The lashes – two from an Indian on one side, then a question; two from the other side and the question: oh, God, what was the question? Guns – guns on *Prinz Ludwig* smashing into *Curie*'s bridge. The confident, supercilious tones of the police lieutenant merging with the confident, fretful voice of Lieutenant-Commander Bowyer.

Dettner awoke. He was lying on his stomach, his hands up on the pillow as they had been tied up on the wall, the sweat was cold on his face and on his chest. Outside, he could hear the voices of the girl watchkeepers calling to the driver. About half past midnight. In the dark silence of the night the voices were fresh and clear. And reassuringly normal. The hot glare of the Calcutta sun, as he was brought out of the earth-floored cell still lingered in his mind; the immaculate ship with Peter and 'Bunny' Hare and the O.O.W., the Quartermaster in spotless whites, himself unwashed and unshaven, dazed at the happenings of the previous 24 hours, his shirt and trousers crumpled and dirty, the Nilssen Line cap and his instinctive attempt to salute the quarterdeck. He snapped on the light to destroy the vision.

Outside in the lane the girls saw the light in the upper window of the dockyard building, waved to it cheerfully and went inside the house opposite, to dip mugs into the pan of hot *kai* awaiting them in the galley.

17

Captain Harding came the next morning with Chief Officer Polruthan and Lieutenant Commander Bowyer to see the extent of the damage sustained by the destroyer and the progress made on its repair.

Dettner greeted them in the yard and they walked over to the dock. He had been struggling to digest a wad of documents Mirsch had brought out regarding the proposed European Recovery Programme and how it could affect the financing of the yard. The O.E.E.C. was already established and the Council of Europe was due for its first meeting in Strasbourg next summer. The new plan, named after General Marshall, had arisen after Bizonia, the merging of the British and American zones. To the ex-*Kapitän zur See*, totally non-political, whose life and actions had, to a great extent, been ruled by orders from above, it was like looking into a black hole. In his own job at sea, he was well able to take independent action when it was necessary. But to control the financing and the building-up of trade in the yard was beyond his knowledge. Still – Albrecht had done it during the early twenties, though he had had previous experience.

'You seem somewhat *distrait*, Captain Dettner,' said the Chief Officer who was walking beside him, following Harding and Bowyer. 'And look as if you had a bad night.'

He apologised shortly for his lack of attention and left it at that. He had no intention of discussing either his nightmares or his financial concerns with this young woman – though he did wonder briefly whether or not Mirsch had sufficient coffee if they all came back to the office.

Jenna came to the yard again on the third day. The dock had

been filled when she got there and from the car she could see the ship floating proudly in her element again. Her officers and part-crew, who were to take her down-river to embark the rest of the ship's company who would be marched from the barracks, were aboard and Bowyer would be taking delivery of his ship back from dockyard hands. She did not go down to the dock but stood watching, visualising the sliding open of the gates to the river, the casting off of the four moorings by which the ship had been secured. The blocks and cradles which had supported her would have been retrieved and she would be under her own power, free to go back to sea.

She could see Dettner on the river-end of the dock, supervising her departure. She knew very well that part of him would be going down-river with her and her heart melted with pity.

The ship slid out into the river and swung round to start her journey. She gave three triumphant whoops and Dettner raised his hand in acknowledgement. Then he turned and came back towards the office.

Jenna went up the steps and found Mirsch. She gave him a jar of coffee.

'We seem to have drunk rather a lot of yours, lately,' she said and sat down in an armchair.

'I think we shall have to give you a new sign, Captain Dettner,' she said, as he came in. 'By Appointment to the Admiralty, London. Have you got the papers handing her back to the Navy?'

'Yes.' He pulled them from his pocket. 'Will you take them?'

She held out her hand for them and glanced through them. Signatories: Henry Bowyer, Lt-Cdr; H.G. Dettner.

'It was a good job,' she said. 'I wish I could think they would recognise it in some way.'

'It would save me a lot of headaches if they did,' he said and sat down.

'You look absolutely knackered,' she said, shocked.

He did not recognise the term and turned his head to look at her, enquiringly. She noted he had not called to Mirsch and that he seemed a bit surprised when the steward brought them coffee. She also noted Mirsch's quick glance at her, to indicate its origin.

'It's time you had a break,' she said and drew a reluctant smile.

'Yes? Who runs the yard? Where should I go? Home?'

'I'm sorry,' she said. 'That was a thoughtless remark. Anyway, I was to give you Captain Harding's compliments and invite you to the Base, tomorrow evening.'

He was silent, considering. Had they no idea? It would have given him a great deal of pleasure to be a wardroom guest again. But he had many uniforms from full dress to tropical kit and some civilian wear, mostly of London tailoring, but also mostly of 1937 and earlier vintage. The fact that his naval pay had abruptly ceased and his more recent earnings had gone to support his family had left him with nothing very suitable for a visit to an RN mess.

'Please thank Captain Harding and convey my regrets,' he said, shortly.

She gave him a long look but accepted his refusal without question. When she informed Captain Harding, as she handed over the completed documents, he swore softly. She asked him why.

'We've been somewhat insensitive,' he said. 'You wouldn't go to the WRNS wardroom in your battle blouse, would you?'

'Bloody hell!' said Jenna, savagely and inelegantly. 'We can't rectify that one, can we?'

Dettner, however, did take a break. He took a day off on the sixth of December, to go over to Oldenburg with a Christmas gift for his nephew. Anton Wessel and the boy were out and Isolde welcomed her brother rather ungraciously. She had quite a reasonable two-bedroomed apartment but grumbled at having had to leave the Ulsdorf house and its garden. Hans, himself, had no value for her now that he was stripped of his rank and uniform. He was thankful to escape and return to the dockyard.

The work, at least, continued to come in. A number of docks had been filled in, as in Kiel and shipyards destroyed in the first flush of victory, but it was increasingly obvious that the German economy would have to be put on its feet before the drain on Allied resources became too great. However, the Navy continued to spread its sheltering wing over the old U.O. dockyard and the job numbers climbed into double figures. The Marshall aid programme, which was later to cover the Berlin airlift and defeat the Russian blockade, rumbled into action and industrial production began to flourish.

The New Year was well into its stride when a frigate, having met some exceptionally heavy seas, crept into Fremenshaven with most of her superstructure shattered and was directed up-river to the German yard, much to her Captain's freely-expressed annoyance. He had left most of his crew to go into barracks and was more than displeased to learn that the rest of them, together with himself and his officers, were to vacate the vessel and sign her over into dockyard hands.

'How do we know everything's going to be safe with fucking krauts all over the place?' he demanded of his Number One as they came on to the quayside.

She was tied up in the basin and the leather-jacketed man who had supervised their mooring did not appear to understand what the C.O. had said. Lt-Cdr Philp was a dark-haired man whose jowls looked perpetually to be in need of a shave. He was one of those unfortunates who had climbed by merit but without any of the social graces to smooth his way. He was good-looking enough, well-built and fit and over-convinced of his own attraction. He turned to Dettner and spoke in the loud, carefully-enunciated way that he felt led to understanding of English by a foreigner.

'I was told an Engineer Officer would meet us,' he said.

Dettner nodded. He had seen Jenna's car arrive and led the two officers to the office. She was there as they went in, spreading out some plans on the chart table. Philp looked from her to Dettner.

'Sorry!' he said. 'Didn't know you had a date.' Then he saw the plan. 'Here!' Where did that come from? They're plans of my ship.'

'Captain Philp and Lieutenant Craven,' said Dettner, gently. 'Engineer Chief Officer Polruthan.'

Philp's eyes went to the straps on her shoulders.

'Sorry,' he mumbled again. 'They didn't say you—'

'That I was a Wren officer?' she said. 'You will address me as Ma'am. And Captain Dettner, here, as Sir. Now, let us look at these plans and see where the damage is. After that, you can go back to the Base in my car.'

'Surely we'll check over the ship with you—Ma'am?'

'No. We shan't need you for that. The ship is in Captain Dettner's charge now.'

'But what the blazes does he know about warships?' He jerked his head at *Prinz Ludwig*'s photograph. 'Don't tell me that was built here – Ma'am.'

'No,' she said, mildly. 'And moderate your tone, please, Philp.'

She spoke to Dettner in German and they turned to the plan. He took up a pencil and swiftly sketched in the areas of damage that he had observed from the exterior of the ship. She looked at Philp.

'Is that it?' she said and he grudgingly agreed.

'There's a lot of internal damage, of course. But our P.O. got the electrics working again.'

'Good. Thank you, gentlemen. I've told my driver where to take you.' She watched them depart and turned back to Dettner. 'I'm sorry you had to suffer that churl,' she said. 'They come like that, occasionally.'

'They can't all be clean-cut empire builders,' he agreed, teasing her.

'Do not take the mickey, Captain,' she said, severely. 'Come on. We'll take a tour of his precious ship.'

Philp, however, remained highly indignant. He found himself sharing a dram or two with the Base Commander (E), a Scotsman, who had passed out of Keyham in the days when engineers were known as 'plumbers' and not quite the thing. Several other members of the wardroom had gathered.

'How was I to know the Engineer Officer was a bloody woman?' Philp moaned. 'And as for leaving my ship with a load of krauts – I only hope the damned fellow knows what he is doing.'

'Do ye mind, laddie, when the war ended,' said Commander (E) looking into his empty glass reminiscently, 'and all the C.O.s of German ships at sea were ordered to surrender to the nearest Allied port? There was one sent a signal to Admiralty, London, saying he was proceeding Wilhelmshaven and giving his expected date and time of arrival. He was in the South Atlantic at the time. He was the Captain of the heavy cruiser *Prinz Ludwig* – the man who is repairing your frigging little frigate. I've always enjoyed that story – and I admire the man who sent that signal even more now. Yes, I'll have the other half, thanks.'

18

Hans Gerhardt Dettner was not a sentimental man. He was the product of his handsome, bullying father and the stiff-backed, unloving woman who had borne him. His life, until he had got to the higher ranks of his profession, had been hard. But his early initiation into fear and brutality had given him a deeper understanding of his fellow men. As Jenna had said to Harding, he had held his crews; the men liked, admired and followed him.

Philp's attitude had not worried him and he had left it to the Chief Officer, Philp's superior, to discipline him which she had done, quietly. He had accepted, now, his present position and his only softening was when he looked at the picture of *Prinz Ludwig* and knew his heart was still with her.

Financially, the yard was doing well. It still came under the local supervision of the Military Governor and was looked on benevolently by the Navy who monitored progress. Which meant Jenna still came to Ulsdorf.

The dreadful finality of the Potsdam decree that all German forces be completely and finally abolished seemed to be easing under the Russian cold war threat and it became increasingly obvious that Germany must soon be able to play some part in her own defence. The French, who had not been invited to the Potsdam talks, were also being difficult but the buzz was of the establishment of a new parliament with a western zone capital in Bonn.

These higher political matters did not interest Dettner greatly. It was the future effect that concerned him. Despite the thirties' depression, Albrecht had flourished up to the outbreak of war and the U.O. Line had held assets in London which, until now, had been frozen. With some assistance from Chalmers these had now been released and Dettner was toying with the idea of leasing back a couple of ships and reopening trade. He was browsing through one of Albrecht's files at his desk when Jenna came in. He rose, with his usual courtesy, but she waved him back and sank into an armchair.

'Philp and Craven will be coming out shortly,' she said. 'I understand the bridge and wheelhouse have been rebuilt. Are you satisfied? Because you may be sure Philp will pick on anything to complain about.'

'The job is not completed yet,' he said. 'But what has been done is up to standard. We have three more days to the estimated completion date.'

'Oh, well – that's a bit of a let-out,' she said.

He regarded her, amused.

'Are you suggesting we shall need excuses?'

She looked up, sharply, realising what she had inferred.

'Hell – I didn't mean it like that,' she said, laughing.

He leaned back in his chair. It was four months now since she had first walked into the office with the young Blair and startled him as a woman engineer.

'Tell me,' he said, 'is it permitted to ask a Wren officer out to dinner?'

'I don't see why not?' she said and added, innocently, 'Have you been visiting the Wrens' Quarters?'

She saw the swift laughter in his eyes as he acknowledged the hit.

'I was aiming rather higher than that,' he said. 'I think our visitors are here.'

Philp and his Number One came into the office, caps off, greatcoats on, for the February morning was sharp and clear. Jenna had not taken hers off. Philp said good morning and rather hesitantly addressed Jenna.

'Is it OK if we visit the ship, Ma'am?'

She returned the greeting and spoke to Dettner in English.

'May I take them to see progress, Captain?'

'Please do. Hoche will be there. He is rewiring.'

'I didn't know he spoke English,' said Philp, defensively, as they crossed the yard.

'Don't worry,' said Jenna, kindly, 'he's used to dealing with young officers.'

She came back to the office alone.

'It was almost too much for him to find Hoche spoke English too,' she said, chuckling.

'Oh, we are a very clever nation,' Dettner said, dryly. 'What are the chances of running a couple of ships, again?'

She sat down, staring at him, speculatively.

'I will ask,' she said. 'But I would say – perhaps not this year.'

He put Albrecht's file back into the tall cupboard.

'We still have some tonnage,' he said. 'Why is it all so slow? The French object, the Russians object. Don't you and the Americans have any say in the matter?'

Jenna struggled not to smile but he saw it in her eyes and returned to his desk with an exasperated laugh at his own impatience.

'You are going too fast, Captain,' she said. 'Not everyone has put the war so firmly behind them.'

'No. But I had little choice.' He did not sit down again but stood looking at a list on the desk. 'I get enquiries from people who shipped with my father. They ask when we shall be able to restore commerce abroad. I do not know – I only did some gun-running for a Danish line.'

Jenna got up, laughing.

'Unwittingly, I believe,' she said. 'I must go.'

'So may I invite you to dinner? Tonight? Tomorrow?'

'I would like that,' she said. 'Tonight. The Wren Officers' Quarters are at the Naval Base.'

So that evening she found herself with a double dilemma – the eternal question of what to wear when out of uniform and the more personal question of what the hell she was up to. As one part of her reviewed her civilian wardrobe the other part was arguing: he's an ex-enemy naval officer, now following his father as a dock master – a small voice interpolated 'Who was owner of a thriving shipping line' – about whom you know little except that he is ten years older than you ... and makes you go bloody weak at the knees. Yes, he has charming manners but so have most of the Base workers, it's just Continental; yes, he has a taut, hard body but he's also as hard as nails. Yes, all right, I'm going out to dinner with him but that doesn't mean anything – does it?

She chose the inevitable little black number – a sleeveless dress in case there was dancing which had a softly-cut long-sleeved jacket for dining.

She was just pulling on a loose overcoat when the Quarters Petty Officer knocked on the door and said 'There's a Captain Dettner for you, Ma'am,' and her eyes suggested a measure of awed respect.

He was awaiting her in the lobby, perfectly at ease and studying the framed prints of old sailing vessels that adorned the walls. She paused at the head of the stairs and saw that for all his apparent slight build he had good shoulders and the immaculately-tailored jacket of his dark suit hung beautifully from them.

He heard her and turned to look at her as she came down the stairs and his eyes appreciated what he saw.

'I am not sure how I should compliment a Chief Officer,' he told her as she gave him her hand.

'I am not a Chief Officer tonight,' she found herself saying and mentally shook herself. He gave her a delicate spray of spring flowers and the cynical part of her mind said, 'H'm! Practised.' while she expressed her pleasure and pinned it to her coat. 'I know you are Hans,' she said. 'I'm Jenna.'

'I know,' he said, ruefully. 'But I did not know how to pronounce it. Zhenna? Unusual.'

'No. Cornish,' she said and, laughing, threw her cynic away.

He had a car outside and, having disposed of her evil genie, she demanded blithely, 'Have you come into a fortune?'

'In a way,' he replied, amused. 'The U.O Line assets are being released – and the rate of exchange is very favourable!'

Thereafter, Jenna submitted herself to the pleasures of the evening. She didn't know where they dined: it was softly-lit, had an unobtrusive orchestra, no cabaret and no dance floor. She remarked on it.

'No. This is for conversation,' he said. 'We can go on to dance if you wish.'

The menu was in French which he seemed to speak as well as

English. She told him to order for her but he deftly extricated himself from that one.

'Not this time,' he said. 'I do not know your tastes, yet.'

They went on to a nightclub to dance and got back to the WRNS Quarters at a respectable two o'clock. Jenna went to her cabin, sat on her 'navy-iron' bedstead and reviewed her thoughts.

'I hear you were on the tiles last night, Jenna,' said Captain Harding when she entered his office, next morning.

'Yes, sir,' she agreed. 'I didn't know one could still get food like that, here.'

'Black market, I suppose,' he grunted. 'Old man Dettner was well-known here. His son would know where to go.'

'What happened to the old man?'

'We were sinking some of the old ships – there were three U.O. Line ones.' Harding lit his pipe. 'The explosives expert would plant the scuttling charges and then scamper back to the tug and get clear. Old Albrecht hid himself on one of the ships and went down with it. It was the second time he'd lost most of his fleet.'

'Poor man!'

'The thing was,' said Harding, slowly, 'his son was skippering the tug.'

'Did he know that Albrecht was aboard?'

'Not till he saw him on the bridge – and it was too late to get him off.'

'Why was – Captain Dettner – skippering the tug?'

'He took a lot of jobs when he came back here – to support his mother and sister. The tug went to Poland as part of reparations. That's when he took *Neumark* to Calcutta and found he was gun-running. I think it shook him up quite a bit.'

'I should think it would,' said Jenna, thoughtfully.

None of this had come out in their conversation at dinner last night. Most of that conversation, she recalled, had centred on her and her family and Cornwall and Devon. Hard as nails, she thought. What else could he be?

'Would you have him invited to a Guest Night, please?' she said to Harding.

'All right,' he growled. 'Mind you, I don't know what I'm letting you get yourself into!'

19

Jenna went to the Ulsdorf yard three days later for the handover of the repaired frigate. It conformed totally to the original plans and she could not think that Philp would find cause for complaint. Nor did he. She and Dettner saw the trim little ship on its way down-river and walked back to the office.

'They were the ships that destroyed the U-boats,' remarked Dettner.

'Yes. Yes, I know – they were designed for it.'

'And now, what?' he mused. 'Laid up? Decommissioned?'

Jenna laughed.

'We really cannot start wars just to keep the Navy at sea,' she said.

'No. But your Navy still has a role.' He called to Mirsch and they sat down. Jenna recognised with pleasure that he was relaxed and ready to talk with her. 'You have still Hong Kong, Singapore, Colombo – still many places to show the flag.'

'Not much longer,' she said. 'The days of Empire are numbered. As with India, we shall be giving the Colonies self-rule. Hong Kong is all right for another 50 years – 1997 the lease runs out. After that, who knows?' She paused to take coffee from Mirsch and then drew a white envelope from her pocket. 'We have a Guest Night once a month. Will you come to the next one? I have an invitation here for you from Captain Harding.'

He was silent for some moments.

'Are you sure?' he said at last. 'A German guest in a British mess?'

'If you're thinking you might be received as the U-boatmen received us,' she said, 'the situation is quite different.'

'Yes. The roles are reversed, are they not?'

'You mean you are the loser coming amongst the magnanimous victors?' she flashed. 'For God's sake, Hans, we are not like that.'

He held out his hand for the envelope. It was addressed to Herrn H.G. Dettner and the card within invited Herr Dettner to attend the Guest Night at HMS *Blackavon* and to RSVP to the Mess President thereof. Black tie. Jenna watched him as he read it.

'You will be there?' he asked.

'Yes. Captain Harding, of course. Commander (E) is rather a fan of yours. And rumour has it that Vice-Admiral Chalmers will be visiting at the time. But do not tell me that you are shy of entering a mess without someone to hold your hand!'

'Chalmers is Vice-Admiral now?' he said, evading her last remark. 'And why should Commander (E) be a fan?'

'Because he says you sent an impertinent signal to Admiralty.'

'Not at all! It informed them of my destination and time of arrival. It was no good informing the Russians in Berlin.'

'I must go,' she said and stood up. He got up, too and gave her the documents for the frigate. She paused, smiling. 'You, Herr Dettner, have the cheek of the devil,' she said gently.

The Guest Night at HMS *Blackavon*, which Dettner was as yet unaware was a Dartmoor stream, took place ten days later, the first Friday in March. Jenna, looking around the ante-room, found a medley of guests, no civilian wives, some Army males and females and a couple of civilian administrators in dinner jackets. The Navy in their mess undress and the Army with the broad red stripe down their trousers and the red, blue-faced short jackets made colourful displays. She was one of six WRNS officers in long blue skirts and short blue jackets with soft shirts and the black tabs at the collar. She was not normally conscious of her appearance but she knew that the kit enhanced her slenderness and, indeed, the Commander RNVR who had accompanied her on the dockland bar escapade remarked on it as he brought her a drink.

'You are looking very charming tonight,' he said. 'Any guest?'

'No,' she said, 'I've not invited anyone. Have you?'

'No. We shall have to console each other.' Commander Howard looked to the door. 'Hullo, do I recognise this one?'

Jenna watched Captain Harding – himself, by reason of his rank, a guest – and Dettner come in, met the keen, blue gaze for a fraction of a second and saw them go to meet the Mess President, the Base Commander.

'You should do,' she replied to Howard. 'He rescued us from that pub we went slumming to.'

'Oh, Lord, yes. Some U-boatmen started singing. But he's German!'

'Yes,' she said, mockingly. 'Do you think the mess will survive?'

'I'm not sure that he will,' muttered Howard. 'We've got a couple of Canadian navy here – he is the one who sank *Curie*, isn't he?'

'Interesting!' said Jenna. 'Ah, here's the Admiral, so that should be the lot.'

Vice-Admiral Chalmers came in, accompanied by the NO i/c and attended by his flag lieutenant, a very smart young man ready to pick out and bring over anyone the great man might wish to speak to.

However, Chalmers threw that overboard and having been welcomed by the President he made a beeline for Harding and his companion.

'Evening, Harding – hullo, Dettner, glad to see you here. I've messages from Peter and Kate, when we've got a minute – and from young John, of course. Catch you later.'

He passed on for a word with the Army Major and his Flags followed, mentally noting who was to be recalled later.

They went into dinner, the RM band playing soft music in the lobby, making a nice background to the buzz of conversation. Dettner found himself between Harding and Jenna, though whether that was considerate or strategic he did not know. She had Howard on her other side and briefly reacquainted them with each other.

'How long since you were in a British wardroom?' she asked him as the steward put soup before them.

'Apart from the gunboat when Peter Sillifant came over,' he said, 'not since Seahaven in 1938.'

'How are you enjoying it?'

'I'm terrified,' he said. 'Particularly as I nearly arrived after the Admiral.'

'Not like you to mistime things,' she teased him.

'No,' he agreed, readily. 'But I had to stop to ask which was the entrance for the wardroom.'

She smiled in disbelief because the gate sentry would have directed him. Soup plates were removed and, it being only a simple post-wartime meal, the roast and vegetables were served. Jenna turned dutifully to Howard, and Harding claimed Dettner's attention. The meal proceeded on its way and Jenna returned to her other neighbour. She noted he refused the pudding and was drinking little. Then the band stopped playing and the President called for the Loyal Toast.

'You drink to the King, Captain Dettner?' she murmured as the bandmaster was called in for his glass of port.

'Surely, anyone still with a crown these days deserves a toast,' he rejoined.

Coffee was served in the ante-room and conversation became general. Jenna was glad that because of the absence of civilian women the usual game of general post – bringing up officers for a chat in turn – was not being played. She and Howard were recalling the bar episode and asking after the U-boat officers with Dettner when one of the Canadian officers who had been sitting opposite at the dining table came up.

'Did I hear you called Captain Dettner?' he asked. 'Still call yourself Captain?'

'I don't,' said Dettner, equably. 'Some people are kind enough to do so.'

The other Canadian, possibly fearing some mention of the troopship, came up also. He was not much more tactful.

'Say, what do you think of this idea of rearming you? Do we trust you fellers now?'

'No. If I were you I'd not trust us an inch.'

'Oh, come on, sir!' said Howard. 'Be serious. If you're rearmed because of the Russian threat, you would fight them again?'

Dettner turned it aside, smiling. He wanted to say that was what Dönitz had asked before the bloody Americans stood back and let the Russians advance across half of Germany. How had the war been won by these people – by a mixture of integrity and naïvety and a blind faith in themselves? He found the Flag Lieutenant at his elbow.

'The Admiral's compliments. He would like to speak with you, please, sir.'

Chalmers greeted him with a grin.

'I thought you might need rescuing,' he said. 'Now, young John came up with his mother to visit Peter the other day and he told me particularly to say *Guten Abend, Herr Kapitän* and that he will be learning German at his new school.' They talked for a bit about Peter and Kate and Dartmoor and Chalmers remarked on the fact that the Blackavon after which the Base was named, flowed through part of the moor. The Flags brought up some other recipient of the Admiral's favour and Harding claimed Dettner and introduced the Scottish Commander (E).

After some discussion on *Prinz Ludwig*'s diesel power, Commander (E) said, 'But tell me, why did ye bring her home and give her up? Why didn't ye scuttle her?'

'In the South Atlantic?'

'But you cud've gone –' Commander (E) wondered where he could have gone where the ship would not have been interned or taken for reparations.

'To Montevideo – and shot myself?' suggested Dettner, rather brutally for he was beginning to feel a little battered. 'No, I was not brave enough. It was better to make a peaceful passage home.'

'Aye, laddie, I daresay.'

Commander (E) left them and Harding guided Dettner to the bar.

'I think we could do with a drink,' he said and signalled to a steward. 'The Admiral tells me you want to get some ships again,' he went on as whisky was brought to them.

'Yes. I understand Hamburg-Amerika are negotiating for one with government aid. Is it a possibility?'

Harding regarded him for a moment, then started to laugh.

'With you, I would say anything's a possibility,' he said. 'We'll go into it. Ah! The Admiral's leaving.'

The departure of the Admiral and the NO i/c meant that lesser fry were now free to make their farewells and thanks to the Mess

President and leave, preferably in order of seniority. So, Harding being equal in rank to the NO i/c, he and his guest did so. They paused in the lobby to talk and Dettner thanked the Engineer Captain for arranging the invitation to the Guest Night.

'Oh, it was Jenna who asked me to,' said Harding, grinning. 'She could have done it herself, as a member of the Mess. Too shy, I expect.'

Too shy, thought Dettner as he went to his car. Unlikely!

Jenna, seeing them go, thought he had coped pretty well. But wasn't that what all good C.O.s had to do? Take and deal with every situation as it arose, taking all responsibility for what occurred in the ship, never flinching, never giving way – publicly at least. She saw the picture he had stuck on the wall, which had disappeared after Captain Sillifant's visit. Laughing, with the laughing crew behind him, self-assured, confident – oh, for God's sake, Jenna, pull yourself together.

She looked round. The Base Commander and Commander (E) were the seniors present, equal to her. She decided she wanted to go to bed.

20

Chalmers and Harding were old shipmates and they were together in the Engineer Captain's office the next morning, having a good gossip and entertaining Jenna who had been instructed to stand by as they were going out to Ulsdorf later.

'What's out there at the moment?' Chalmers asked her.

'Three merchantmen. Two in the basin and one in the dry dock,' she said.

'There's a big enough workforce for that?'

'If it's juggled a bit. You know, sir – welders on one, electrical gang on another, so on.'

'And what about the U.O. Line? Can Dettner handle that, too?'

'I would think so, sir.'

'Can he afford to buy in ships?' asked Harding.

'He'd get Government assistance, of course, like HAPAG. But now the U.O. assets are being unfrozen he's quite a rich man – in several places. Even Calcutta, I expect!' Chalmers chuckled. 'When old Albrecht's will was proved I managed to get the London bankers to unfreeze – that's how he got his tailor out here.'

'Yes – I fancied last night that dinner jacket had a London stamp.'

Chalmers eyed Harding's comfortable bulk.

'Got the figure to carry it well, too,' he remarked.

Like a couple of old women nattering, thought Jenna as the Leading Wren opened the door to admit the steward with coffee.

They were just about finishing it when, over at Ulsdorf, Hoche, the electrical foreman, walking along the dockside, tripped and went into the river. At his despairing yell, two of his gang who had been following, hurled a lifebelt after him and shouted for help.

Dettner, at the edge of the basin, swung round and saw the bobbing head and frantically waving arm in the grey, murky water. For a moment he was paralysed as head and arm multiplied until there were hundreds of them floating there. Then he kicked off his shoes and took a header off the quayside. He was further downriver but the current was taking Hoche down and he should be able to intercept him and tow him into the basin.

When Chalmers, Harding and Jenna arrived they met Mirsch just running down the office steps. He checked when he saw them, bowing and addressing Jenna hurriedly in German.

'He thinks somebody's in the river,' she translated tersely and they followed the man across the yard.

At the top of the steps leading down into the basin a couple of men were pumping Hoche free of the water he had swallowed. Several other men stood, watching. Dettner was sitting on the quayside, his forehead resting on his updrawn knees. As they neared he twisted over on to his stomach and spewed filthy water back into the basin. Harding went over swiftly, knelt down and applied helpful pressure on his back and then lifted him to his feet.

Dettner thanked him, realised who it was and said, 'Oh, God!' in blank dismay.

He turned, saw Chalmers and Jenna, wiped his mouth on his soaking shirtsleeve and went over to Hoche. The man was on his feet and volubly grateful.

'Take him home,' said Dettner to the two electricians. 'The rest of you carry on.' He turned to Chalmers. 'I am sorry, Admiral. We don't put on a show like this very often.'

'So I believe,' said Chalmers. 'First entry in the accident book, eh? Has the man far to go home?'

'No. He lives in the village. They will walk him back.'

'Good. You cut along and shift into dry clothes. If you will allow Chief Officer Polruthan to show us around?'

'Yes, of course.'

'Sillifant sent you some whisky,' said Chalmers. 'Tell your steward to collect it from my car. Right. Come on, Chief Officer.'

They did a moderately extended tour to allow time for Dettner to recover himself and walked back to the office when they reckoned the sun was well over the yardarm.

He was studying plans of the ship in dry dock, having showered to get the river stench off his skin and out of his hair and was dressed in a blue shirt and khaki drill slacks belted around his middle. A chest and stomach hard and flat as a washboard, thought Jenna. She had never seen him put out of countenance before but he was fully himself now.

They drank Peter's whisky.

'Help to kill off the river bugs,' suggested Harding, blithely.

It was not the bugs, thought Dettner, it was the head, the bobbing heads that he had to shut out now. At least, once Mirsch had gone, there was no one to hear at night if he cried out at the accusing arms that waved at him from the heaving water. He lifted his gaze from the whisky in his glass and looked straight into the compassionate eyes of Chalmers and knew that the Admiral knew. It came stupidly into his mind to say, 'One less – I have redeemed one,' but he did not speak.

Saturday afternoons and Sundays saw only a small emergency squad at the yard, who also acted as watchmen until the nightguards came on. As weekends meant nothing to the WRNS watchkeepers, their cars continued to run and, by his own choice, Mirsch came out too. Which was as well.

Dettner had not expected to have a good night. Normally now, the nightmares were infrequent unless something triggered them. The multiplication of Hoche's head and waving arm into the hundreds thrown into the sea when *Curie* sank had made too clear a vision not to provoke a night-time replay. He read for a while, hoping to fill his mind with other pictures and when he heard the midnight watchkeepers return, turned off the light and went to sleep. That, in itself, was not difficult – he was tired enough. But the ensuing dreams that gripped him and tore him apart were prolonged and vicious. He awoke at last to pitch blackness and a silence broken only by his own rasping breath. His watch told him it was three o'clock and, as he dragged himself out of the horror that still clung, he realised he was feeling most unwell. Because he was so rarely ill, it was all the more apparent.

Otto Mirsch found him at half past seven, burning with fever and just sufficiently conscious to recognise Mirsch's arrival.

The ex-Petty Officer was a phlegmatic man but he had a devotion to this man whom he still recognised as his Captain. He took in the situation, got a bowl of tepid water and sponged down the burning body, smoothed out the crumpled undersheet, found more pillows and left Dettner, propped up and breathing more easily, while he went out and summoned an ex-mate of his who had been a sickberth attendant and now worked on the yard. Together they strove, partly by instinct, partly by the sheer desire to bring ease and comfort. To their minds Dettner had rescued them from despair and worked unstintingly to keep the yard going and themselves in employment. He had unhesitatingly gone to the aid of their mate in the river and now they had to save him from the consequences. So they cooled him when he burned, wrapped him warmly when he shivered uncontrollably and gently fed him with sips of water, of fruit juice and broth.

About mid-afternoon, they saw the beads of sweat break out on his forehead and run down his face and looked at each other with satisfaction. They sponged him off, laid him back on the pillows to sleep and went to make themselves mugs of tea.

When Dettner awoke, he found himself propped on pillows, the light in the passage outside shining through his open door. It was just after seven o'clock in the evening so he called to Mirsch and was startled to find he could barely raise a whisper. However, the steward appeared and looked him over with an air of proprietorial satisfaction.

'I think you have saved my life, Mirsch,' Dettner said.

'Well, then, sir, that's a life for a life, isn't it?' Mirsch propped him a little higher and put a mug of broth in his hands. 'I called Weiss off the yard to give me a hand, him having been an SBA. I hope that was all right, sir?'

Dettner, holding the mug in both hands and sipping from it gratefully, thought it could hardly have been more all right. A life for a life? So did that discount the one he thought he had redeemed? Somehow, it didn't matter any more.

'I am more than thankful,' he said. 'I'll see Weiss in the morning. It's nearly time you went, isn't it?'

'I shall be here tonight, sir,' said Mirsch, matter-of-factly. 'Weiss is letting my wife know I shan't be back.'

This expression of loyalty and the feeling of relief that he would not be alone that night made Dettner want to weep. He suppressed the desire firmly, putting it down to his weakened state.

'Thank you, Mirsch,' he said. 'That is very kind.'

Mirsch went back to his galley, hiding a satisfied smile. The Captain was nearly back on the bridge.

In the morning, when Harding telephoned, Dettner was at his desk. He had seen the three foremen in the office, satisfied himself as to Hoche's well-being and thanked Weiss. Mirsch had brought him hot rolls, honey and coffee and apart from some weakness and a harsh cough, he felt reasonably well.

'Just calling to find out how your foreman is,' said Harding. 'Recovered from his dip?'

'Yes. I have seen him this morning and he tells me he has no ill effects.'

'Splendid. And you?'

'I am well.'

'Good. You'll be glad to hear that Admiral Chalmers was very impressed. He wants to keep you on the list for any repairs to our ships. Maybe refits, later. And I should think you might start looking for that ship you want.'

'That is good news. I have the ship in mind and a master for her.'

Harding chuckled.

'You don't let the grass grow, do you, Dettner?' he commented.

'Right. I'll be in touch.'

Dettner put down the receiver and looked up as Mirsch came in for the breakfast tray. The man poured out more coffee for him and went out with the tray. All was well. The Captain was definitely back in command.

21

Political moves continued to proliferate. In March five powers signed the Brussels Treaty which named Germany as a possible aggressor although it was the Russian threat that had brought the Western Union into being. In April, common defence measures were agreed and Field Marshal Montgomery became chairman of a military organisation. The Russian objections to a Federal German Government led to their walking out of the Allied Control Council and, later, out of the Berlin *Kommandatura*. The blockade of Berlin and the subsequent air lift meant the Cold War was in full flight. Hans Dettner, struggling to absorb these shifting developments and work out how they would affect the U.O. yard could only hope that rearmament of his country would be advanced and they might achieve at least a small fleet.

The summer was hot. Jenna, making a routine visit to Ulsdorf, found most of the workforce in shorts and singlets. She herself had put on navy linen slacks and a short-sleeved uniform shirt with her rank badges on the shoulders. She found Dettner coming out of the pumping control house on the side of the dry dock, where a freighter was secured in the descending water. He, also, was in short navy shorts with bare feet thrust into leather sandals. She thought, involuntarily, well, thank God he doesn't wear socks with sandals – that would have been too much of a culture shock. Unlike the men, he had on a loose, white shirt. He greeted her with satisfaction.

'Good. I want you to see this ship when the dock is empty. We have an hour.' He glanced at the watch strapped to the underside of his wrist. 'Come back to the office.'

She went with him, wondering, and he disappeared into his

quarters, calling to Mirsch. She found some newspapers spread on the chart table, detailing pacts and treaties and could understand his concern and, probably, confusion. He came back into the office, having exchanged his navy shorts for drill slacks and with car keys in his hand. She allowed him to hurry her down the steps and into his car and out into the road before she spoke.

'It's lucky I drove myself out here,' she said. 'Or we would have had a service driver wasting time and money.'

'No – he would have had to wait while the dock emptied.'

'You realise I am on duty?'

'You have a lunch break?'

'Yes, of course.'

'I may take you out to lunch?'

Jenna started to laugh.

'You appear to be doing so,' she pointed out.

They went out beyond the village of Ulsdorf to a small inn, surrounded by the shade and coolness of woods. They had homemade bread, cheese, apples and ice-cold beer, outside, under the spreading arms of an ancient tree. Jenna regarded the man with new eyes: this setting did not accord with the efficient, hard-as-nails character he normally displayed.

She acknowledged the innate courtesy which had made him change from shorts into clean drill trousers when shorts could well have seemed suitable for a brief rural interlude. Why, she wondered, could foreign men wear shorts so naturally when Englishmen seemed unable to do so? She thought of the naval, white uniform shorts, down to the knee with white socks up to the knee and the self-conscious couple of inches of knobbly flesh between.

Dettner, relaxed in the wooden, armed chair, watched the sun through the leaves dappling her dark curls and wondered what were her thoughts to cause that little twist of amusement on her lips. She had left her tricorne in the car and with the white shirt opened at her throat and her eyes withdrawn, she looked softened and gentle. She turned her head, met his eyes and let her smile grow.

'What a heavenly place, Hans,' she said. 'You don't need a bath to dream in.'

He laughed at that, got up and went in to pay the innkeeper. When he came she was standing ready.

'The dock will be empty and we are back on duty,' she said. 'Can we come here again?'

The pumping dry of the dock had revealed a sturdy merchant vessel of, she guessed, some 6,000 tons, black-painted, with the anti-fouling on her bottom badly in need of cleaning and renewing. She had a certain grace about her lines and a raking stem. The upperworks were painted buff and the stack was black and buff. Jenna was about to ask Dettner why he particularly wanted her to see it when she saw the name on the bow: *Neumark*.

'You've bought her back,' she said, involuntarily. 'Why, Hans? After Calcutta!'

'She is a good ship. She was a gun-runner. She must redeem herself.'

She stared at him, not sure if he were teasing her.

'You believe ships have souls?' she said.

'Of course they have. Come aboard.'

She was a good ship, Jenna agreed as they toured her. Albrecht had had her built at the beginning of the war so she had been in service for about seven years during which her sailing distances had been curtailed considerably. Her engine room was relatively modern and the engineers' quarters were just above, abaft the funnel. Roomy crews' quarters in the forecastle, five holds and five derricks, at present lowered and unrigged, and five winches. The bridge held wheelhouse, chartroom and wireless cabin, the captain's cabin on the lower bridge and the officers' quarters just below. She visualised the ship on her last voyage to Calcutta – a blue sea under a blue sky. But it had not been *Neumark* that he had seen on that sea but *Prinz Ludwig* in the South Atlantic.

'And trade?' Jenna said. 'Can you get cargoes?'

'We are permitted to export to pay for what we need to import.'

'You sound bitter.'

'As you have said to me – we lost. We must put up with the consequences.'

They were standing on a wing of the bridge and Jenna said, sharply, 'You didn't bring her down from Nilssen's yard, did you?'

Dettner shook his head.

'No. Nilssen sent her down with one of his skippers and a passage crew.'

'Didn't you want a sea trip?'

He put his hands on her shoulders and turned her to face him.

'Jenna, don't push me. Yes. I want to go to sea. But not in her.'

She stared into his thin, set face.

'This hurts you,' she said, quietly. 'Why do you do it?'

'Because I must live.' He let her go and gestured towards the yard. 'And these men must live.'

'And if you can't make a go of it?'

'I must. Will you come tonight to find a skipper for *Neumark*?'

'Where?'

'That bar you went to with Commander Howard. He asked me then for a job – he is one of my father's ex-masters. He must be despairing by now.'

'I thought you were buying a ship so you could get back to sea. I am so sorry. You want to employ this man – to give him the hope that you asked we should give you?'

'I do have some finer feelings,' he said, shortly. 'What time should I come for you?'

'Seven?' she said. 'Good Lord! I must get back. Harding will think I've – deserted.'

She caught herself just in time, realising that she had nearly said 'eloped'. She ran down the bridge ladder and crossed the gangway to the dockside. He did not come with her and she looked back and waved. He was leaning on the bridge rail and watching her and she thought sadly he was where he was happiest – on the bridge of a ship even if it were not the ship he wanted.

Apart from removing the blue ranking sleeves from her shoulder straps, Jenna did not change for the evening's assignation. Nor did he.

'Have you eaten?' he asked her when she greeted him in the lobby.

'No. The officers going on watch at twenty hundred hours are not ready to eat yet so, apart from raiding the kitchen, there's nothing going.'

'We'll find somewhere. I don't think Rudi would rise to anything above sausage and sauerkraut.'

'You know Rudi well?'

'He has been a good friend for many years.'

119

He did not enlighten her any further. Like Kate, even like Peter, though he would have gone to Britannia Royal Naval College at 13 and surely had his eyes opened, Jenna had a sheltered innocence that he would not have shattered for the world. Though whether or not that was a kindness he did not know.

They found a pleasant little cafe with tables out in the sun, which gave them a clean and adequate meal and Dettner decided to leave the car there rather than take it to Rudi's bar. They walked there, found a quiet table and looked round. The merchant skipper was there but he looked far gone. Two of the young U-boatmen were there, subdued and dispirited. Rudi came up.

'I don't know that I can drink any more beer,' said Jenna, apologetically.

'And you don't drink schnapps.' Dettner sighed and looked at Rudi who grinned and went off. When he came back, he carried a bottle of a delicate white wine of the country and two wine glasses.

'Only for my Captain,' he told Jenna in a throaty whisper as he poured it out.

It was lightly chilled and delicious.

'Where are the other young aces?' Dettner asked him.

'Two have gone to Hamburg and got work. One, the little one, jumped into the dock and drowned.'

'And Captain Lausen. Is he usually like this?'

Rudi shrugged.

'Sometimes better, sometimes worse. His wife is dead. You knew his son? He was blown up – lost both legs, has fits. He will be in hospital now, always.'

'I knew Frau Lausen was dead. But the boy – what is he? – twenty?'

'It is war. He was so afraid it would finish before he could get into the Army. He had two weeks of it.'

Dettner nodded.

'Give me ten minutes,' he said. 'Then ask those two lads if they will have a drink with me.' He looked at Jenna and corrected himself with a smile. 'With us. You don't mind?'

'No,' she said. 'You called them "aces". They can't be very old, now. Did they command U-boats?'

'Oh, yes. Often the oldest aboard would be no more than twenty-three. It was a young man's game. But they did not stay young.'

'Everywhere there are young men who have known no youth. We've sent a lot of our young officers to university. I suppose it will give them a chance to unwind.'

'And the young women? Or didn't they suffer?'

'One doesn't think of the women,' she said, slowly. 'I don't know how it compares – a destroyer in the Atlantic – a bombed home, a dead child, loss of husband or prospective husband. It's just women's lot – isn't it?'

He did not comment but looked up at the two young men approaching. They came to rigid attention by the table and Jenna feared for one horrible moment that they were going to throw a Nazi salute. They did not. Dettner introduced them.

'Ex-*Kapitän-Leutnant* Schneider. Ex-*Leutnant* Oppen,' he said. 'Chief Officer Polruthan is a marine engineer with the Royal Navy. Sit down.'

They looked at her with respect as Rudi brought them steins of beer.

'I was engineer in my U-boat,' said Oppen, hopefully.

'Why are you not working?' asked Dettner.

'We tried in Hamburg but there were no ships taking on even junior officers,' said Schneider.

'Nor deckhands?'

'I could have gone as ERA,' said Oppen. 'But I knew about diesels and not much about turbines.'

'You can still learn. I can offer you both jobs but it will have to be as apprentices. Four years and then you can sit for your mate's certificate. Think about it. If you are interested come out to Ulsdorf at 0900 tomorrow. Thank you.'

The young men stood up, bowed stiffly and retreated with their steins.

'How will they get out, tomorrow?' asked Jenna.

'They will walk – as I did.' Dettner signalled to Rudi. 'If you can catch Lausen sober and he can get the drink out of him, tell him to come out to Ulsdorf next week.'

22

The Leading Wren Writer in Captain Harding's office looked up and smiled as Dettner entered. Rather different to the travel-weary man who had arrived from England via Hamburg nearly a year ago.

'Good morning, Captain Dettner,' she said. 'Captain Harding is expecting you.'

She got up and opened the door for him to go through. Harding did not miss the appreciative smile as he thanked her.

'Morning, Dettner,' he said. 'How are things going?'

'Well. But it would help if you could send me one of your Wren writers to do some of the paperwork.'

'You can't have Jane,' retorted Harding with a grin. 'If you want a writer you'll have to get one of your ex-Navy men.'

'A pity. The feminine touch.'

'Dammit – my best Wren comes out often enough.'

For a moment steely blue eyes swept his face and Harding thought: Oho, no cracks about our Jenna, is it?

Dettner handed him a folder.

It contained lists of proposed cargoes to be loaded in *Neumark* and, underneath, prospective return cargoes.

'These will be passed by the proper authorities?' Harding asked.

'Yes. But you still control the docks here. I cannot load at Ulsdorf. My father operated from here and owned a wharf and sheds. When do I get them back?'

'My God, you like jumping the gun, don't you?' Harding picked up the telephone. 'Get me the Port Captain, please. Ah, hullo, Renfrew – I want to come down and take a look at the old

U.O. Line wharf, please. Can do? OK. See you, then.' He looked at Dettner. 'Can you idle for half an hour? Good.'

He pressed his bell. When Jane came in, Jenna followed her in, pausing when she saw that he was already engaged.

'Oh, Jane,' said Harding. 'Captain Dettner wants you for his writer. OK?'

'Yessir,' she said, imperturbably. 'When do I start?'

'Hussy!' he said, laughing. 'Tell them to send us some coffee.'

'Yessir,' and she whipped out.

'If you are busy,' said Jenna, 'I'll come back later.'

'Sit down, woman,' said Harding. 'We are going to idle for half an hour over coffee, and then we're off to see Renfrew. You met him when he was acting harbour master, didn't you, Dettner?'

'Bearded, RNR? Yes. He rescued me from the harbour tug.'

'You knew he spent some months as a deckhand on a tug, Jenna?' said Harding. 'Renfrew found he was a Master Mariner and put him on the ocean-going one.'

The steward brought in coffee. Jenna, silent, understood Dettner's unspoken contempt for the young ex-officers of the U-boats.

'While we have the time,' Harding went on when the steward had gone, 'I might as well put both of you in the picture a bit. From the beginning of next year, we shall be winding down. The Military Government will be replaced by an Allied High Commission. Most of the watchkeeping ratings will go first so you should have your house back by next spring, Dettner. We expect a Parliamentary Council to be set up at Bonn by this autumn.'

'You will frighten me back to sea, if you go on,' said Dettner.

Harding eyed him, shrewdly.

'Don't pretend that you're not fully alive to these developments,' he said. 'I admit some may be precipitated a bit by Russia's attitude. Do you still say, Dettner, as you told that Canadian, that we cannot trust you an inch?'

'Trust us?' Dettner smiled, wryly. 'Why should you? We have been following the same policy ever since Attila made himself supreme in Central Europe in the fifth century.'

'So you think European domination will still be on the agenda?'

'World domination. Why do you think the Kaiser wanted to rule you? Look where your Empire spread. Almost everywhere, if you wanted to be understood, you spoke English.'

'Made you hate our guts?'

'Not at all. We slavered at your feet in envy and adoration. Should we be going?'

Harding got up. He was visibly shaken and took his cap from the hat stand in silence. Dettner made a brief bow to Jenna and preceded him from the room.

Jenna poured herself another cup of coffee and sat down again, her own report pushed aside in her mind. Dettner's cynicism had startled her as much as it had Harding. Another facet to a many-sided man.

She wondered which facet she was to see when she drove to the yard a couple of days later. But he met her at his most efficient and discussed with her the matters she raised until a knock on the office door heralded Lausen. He came in, an ingratiating hand raised to his cap, and was certainly quite sober. It was a hot day and he was carrying his reefer jacket to reveal trousers supported by braces over a not too clean shirt.

Jenna watched blue eyes turn to ice as Dettner switched from the English they had been speaking to give the ex-master a rousting in their own language. It was quite quiet, quite short and quite deadly in tone.

'How dare you come here dressed like that? You are no use to me in this state. If you want to be master of my ship you must have pride – in her and in yourself. Get out and come back when you have found some.' As the man, speechless, opened the door to go, he added in a gentler voice, 'What would Albrecht have wanted?'

Lausen checked as he took that in, then quietly left.

'Pride,' said Jenna, softly. 'But you don't want us to restore pride to your country?'

'Pride?' he repeated, leaning back in his desk chair. 'It is not pride that frightens me but arrogance. My mother was Prussian. Her family were Kaiser's men – *pickelhaube*, waxed moustaches, jackboots – all the things you mocked in your cartoons. It is in me, the need to be on top.' His gaze rested gently on the photograph of *Prinz Ludwig*. 'That is why this yard must succeed. At

Seahaven—' He paused and she watched those tell-tale eyes that John had called 'truthful'. 'I had always to be just ahead of Peter. How young we were then.'

'Before the war,' she said, quietly. 'But you were both Commanding Officers.'

The men were coming up from the dockyard to the restroom on the ground floor at the end of the office block, to get their lunch boxes. Some were singing.

'Good Lord, is it lunch time?' said Jenna, getting up. 'I must go. They sound happy enough.'

Dettner went to the window and looked down at them.

'They are in work,' he said, almost to himself and quoted ' "The men come singing from the fields for they have provided for their own." English proverb,' he added, smiling as Jenna swung round to stare at him. He opened the door for her.

'For someone who went to sea at twelve, you are amazingly well educated,' she observed.

'I had seven years at school,' he pointed out. 'And then the Naval Academy. Also, one learns from reading.'

'Sometimes I think I don't know you at all,' she said as they went down the steps.

'Of course you don't. You see me in my naval greatcoat.' He opened the car door for her. 'And I have worn it for too long to shed it now.'

She got in and wound down the window, a ghost of mischief in her dark eyes.

'But sometimes it comes unbuttoned,' she said and started the engine.

He stepped back, smiling and went back up to the office where Mirsch was placidly setting out the table for his lunch.

Over in London, Vice-Admiral Chalmers perused a departmental memo with some interest before handing it across his desk to Peter Sillifant.

'An old friend resurrected,' he said.

'*Neumark*?' said Peter. 'Engaged in the North Sea tramp trade — U.O. Line! Good Lord! Dettner's bought her back?'

'It seems so. He won't like being restricted to the North Sea or the Baltic — I doubt if he'd touch the Baltic, anyway. She's a bit big for the tramp trade – first voyage next month to Port of London and Hull to discharge and pick up.'

'He wasn't too keen about taking on the yard. I wonder if he'll bring her over himself.'

'Doubt it,' grunted Chalmers. 'He's got his hands full at the yard. Also – I think there could be another attraction to keep him there.'

The other attraction, as a beautiful Sunday morning dawned, fell victim to her own restlessness and desire which led her to a step she should not have taken. Keeping in mind as an excuse the old adage All Work and No Play, she drew a car from the pool and took the familiar road. She had on a light-coloured linen suit with a short-sleeved jacket and pleated skirt, which would surely be acceptable for lunch under a shady tree, and flat-heeled sandals. It was not until she turned the car in through the yard gates – which were, surprisingly, open – and saw Dettner coming down the steps of the office block, that she became aghast at what she had done.

He was wearing the beautifully-tailored navy-blue suit with highly polished naval-type shoes, a white shirt and discreetly-striped blue tie. She realised he was on his way to some appointment and with a twinge of jealousy, wondered with whom. He waited for her to pull up, then opened her door and greeted her formally as she got out. She sought frantically for some excuse for her arrival but could think of nothing even remotely plausible.

'You are obviously going out,' she said, rather foolishly.

He looked over her outfit. She had the feeling that he knew exactly what she had had in mind.

'You had better come too,' he said, briefly and opened the door of his car.

Jenna picked up her shoulder bag and transferred to the other car in silence. Once again she did not speak until they were headed for the little village of Ulsdorf.

'Where are we going?' she asked, rather subdued.

'To church.'

She was stunned into silence again. Then the implications began to unroll in her mind. A village church, the village full of employees at the yard. Herself well known to them as the consulting marine engineer.

'No, Hans!' she exclaimed in panic. 'I can't—!'

'Why not?' he said, brutally. 'Isn't it what you came for?'

Oh, God, thought Jenna, what the hell have I done? It was too late now – they had pulled up on an open space before the little church, people were walking in, bells were tolling. He opened her door and held out his hand and she took it numbly and got out.

'Hold your head up, Chief,' he told her and she heard from his voice that he was laughing at her. She lifted her eyes and was shattered by the look in his. 'The honour of the Navy is at stake.'

She held her head high. She saw Mirsch, she saw Hoche and several others and she walked into the church with the man she knew they regarded as their captain and up the length of it to the principal pew where the Pastor was waiting and was introduced to her.

The service she followed in a dream. Lutheran, she supposed, fairly similar, some hymn tunes familiar. Then she had to face the walk back down to the door and only the Pastor in front of them, everyone else still in the pews, waiting to follow and avidly watching her. Another handshake from the Pastor in the sunshine where she could see that his neatly trimmed beard only partly concealed the scars on his cheek.

Dettner did not make her face any more. He put her in the car, raised a hand to acknowledge some of his workforce, exchanged a word with Mirsch, then got in and drove away.

'You did very well, Chief,' he said, still teasing.

'Please!' she said, on the verge of angry tears. 'I am sorry. I should not have come. It was such a beautiful day.'

'It *is* a beautiful day,' he corrected. 'If I wish to take my – attractive engineer out to lunch and we choose to go to church first, why not?'

23

Jenna knew that, by her rash action that Sunday, she had done something irrevocable. She had laid her cards on the table. He, as yet, had not.

They had gone, as she had hoped, to the Inn in the Woods and they had sat in the rustic chairs at the table under the old tree and had lunch and talked over their wine and lingered over their coffee in the sunshine. He had taken off his jacket, after requesting her permission and, unlike Lausen, revealed a spotless long-sleeved shirt and trousers neatly hugging his flat middle. He had told her that Pastor Müller had been a naval padre and wounded when comforting the dying on the deck of his ship. She told him more of her village down in the Roseland peninsula in Cornwall. He spoke of his visits to Greystone and the incredible view from Grey Tor.

They had idled the afternoon away to a final cup of coffee at about teatime then driven back through Ulsdorf to the yard. He did not ask her to come up to the office and she thanked him politely for a lovely day, got into her pool car and drove away.

She reached the Engineer Captain's office at the same time as Harding on Monday morning and as they went in, the telephone began to ring. He nodded to her to take it and went to hang his cap on the stand but paused as he caught the clear, concise voice of the caller.

'Chief Officer? Dettner. Please tell the Captain there is a ship adrift up-river from here. A small coaster, on fire. I have contacted Commander Renfrew who is sending tugs and fire boats. We will try to stop her here but—' He paused and in the background she could hear the strident blaring of the klaxon. The line went dead.

'All right, I heard,' snapped Harding. 'Call for my car.'

They got out of Fremenshaven and along the two miles of road to Ulsdorf in under ten minutes. As they entered the yard they could see smoke and flame from the blazing ship which appeared to be static. On the river quayside they could see teams of men directing fire hoses on board. As they crossed the yard they could make out jets of water directed from the water cannon on the tugs.

Dettner was squatting on the end of the quay by the entrance to the basin, having a shouted conference with Renfrew who had come up-river in the harbour tug and was standing on the foredeck as the tug swung round in preparation to take the line that the dock staff had managed to secure the vessel with. But Renfrew was not sure if he would do better to tow her right out of the river or to beach her on some low-lying shore lower down the river.

'Beach her,' shouted Dettner. 'She may blow before you get—'

Which she did.

Harding and Jenna stopped dead, feeling the blast as it rolled up towards them. Everyone on the dockside was hurled flat.

'Jenna, get to the phone and call for ambulances. Tell the Base to send a medical team,' said Harding, and began to run towards the flattened men.

Others from the yard ran with him and Jenna threw an anxious look back as she fled towards the office block.

Dettner, having been crouching down, was only rolled over. He rolled back to the edge of the dock and looked down at the tug. Renfrew was spread-eagled on the deck. Two deckhands who had been at the stern to secure the tow-rope were blackened shapes. In the wheelhouse the tugmaster had been flung into the screen and was a mass of blood. The helmsman was not in sight. Dettner sat on the edge of the dock and let himself drop, landing on the deck close to Renfrew. As he did, the Chief Engineer, dripping blood from his forehead, appeared.

'Stand by, Chief,' said Dettner and the man nodded and ducked back to his engines.

The burning vessel was going down now and the tug was being dragged back into the vortex. On the bridge, the helmsman was lying on the deck, clutching his chest and moaning. Dettner rang for full speed and took a quick look round.

One of the fire boats had disappeared, leaving debris and heads in the water. The other was striving not to suffer the fate that had threatened the tug. On the tug's deck, Renfrew was sitting up.

Dettner spun her round and interposed her between the burning hulk and the remaining fire boat which was then able to back off. He could see Renfrew crouching behind the bulwarks to escape the heat and headed for the few survivors from the other boat and held the tug while Renfrew dragged them on board. He then made for the basin, waving to the surviving fire boat to follow.

Jenna, running down the steps from the office, found Pastor Müller getting out of his Beetle.

'I heard the klaxon alarm,' he told her as they hurried to the riverside.

There were three dead there and two obviously dying, beside whom Müller knelt. The ambulances came screaming through the gates and the medical team were running across the yard. A few minutes later, Dettner came across from the basin, calling for medical aid for the men in the tug. Renfrew followed him, rather more slowly, limping painfully.

One of the dying men, an Ulsdorf man, saw Dettner and called out for him. He took Müller's place beside him and Jenna heard the man begging that his family be taken care of. She didn't hear Dettner's gentle reply but she watched the man die and saw the grief on Dettner's face. Müller put out a hand and helped him to his feet.

Quickly and compassionately, the medical teams cleared the carnage. The dead were removed to lie quietly in an empty shed; the injured put into ambulances, the men on the tug and the fire boat brought up from the basin on stretchers, the tugmaster heavily bandaged around the face and head, the helmsman with his smashed ribs strapped. At last only the Surgeon-Commander from the Base, Commander Renfrew, Dettner, Harding and Jenna remained. The fire hoses had dealt with the last remnants of fire as the vessel sank below the dockside and were reeled and stowed. The men left had gone to their work places or to the restroom, no doubt to talk in hushed voices. Müller had gone to see the bereaved families in Ulsdorf.

'Can I leave the tugs here in the basin until I can send down relief crews, Dettner?' asked Renfrew and Dettner nodded.

'You'd better come back with me, Renfrew,' said the Surgeon-Commander. 'We'll see what damage you've done. What about you, Captain Dettner?'

'No, thank you. There's nothing that Mirsch can't patch for me.'

They looked at him. Apart from burns on his left forearm and the side of his face and a partly-shredded shirt which bared the old scars on his upper arm and chest, he appeared relatively physically unscathed.

'All right. Come and see me if anything crops up,' said the Surgeon-Commander and went off with Renfrew.

'I'm not sure where the sun is,' said Dettner. 'But would you wait for me in the office while I see my foremen. Mirsch will see to you.'

Harding and Jenna walked up to the office. At the gates some village people clustered but Müller had taken home the two new widows.

Mirsch brought them coffee which they felt they preferred. Some minutes later, Dettner came in. He seemed still very much in command of himself and of the situation but saddened by the injuries and deaths.

'They were too close,' he said. 'I should have known she would blow.'

'Don't blame yourself,' said Harding. 'You've done a marvellous job.'

'I may come out and see the injured this afternoon? And I must see what the relatives want done with the dead.' For an instant his composure nearly cracked as he added, 'It is much easier to bury them at sea.'

'If Renfrew's fit enough, he'll find out what happened up-river and whose vessel it is. We'll clear the wreck and there'll be compensation, of course – for the families as well.' Harding glanced at Jenna and stood up. 'We'll leave you to get cleaned up. Come in to see me at the Base when you've been to the hospital this afternoon.'

It was late afternoon when a subdued Jane announced Dettner to Captain Harding and he followed her into the office, haggard-eyed, the burn standing out fiercely against his tired face. Harding waved him to a seat.

'Why did I stop that bloody ship at the quay?' he asked as he sat down.

'Because you knew damn well what would happen if she got among the shipping at the port,' said Harding. 'Tea or whisky?'

'Whisky.'

'Have you seen the injured?'

Harding poured generous tots.

'Yes. And the families. Just my men – the tugmen and the fire boats' crews are Renfrew's.' He was wearing a black tie with the navy-blue suit and looked totally drained.

'How are the casualties?'

'What do they say in hospitals? As well as can be expected. I don't think there'll be any more deaths.'

'Well, thank God for that. The tugmaster, fortunately, was very bloody but not too serious. The helmsman got flattened against the wheel and broke six ribs.'

They were silent a while, contemplating the havoc. Then Jenna came in.

'I saw your car,' she said to Dettner. 'It's totally inadequate but I did want to say how desperately sorry I am. Your men – you had such good teams working.'

He nodded.

'The two Ulsdorf men will be buried on Friday,' he said. 'The three from Fremenshaven, I don't know yet.'

He got up wearily, bade them both goodnight and went out. Jenna sat down abruptly.

'Oh – God!' she said, forcefully.

Dettner went back to the yard and sat down in the office. Sunday and Monday. They are carried up to the heaven and down again to the deep. When Mirsch came in, he was sleeping soundly in the armchair.

Two days later, Captain Bailey, the NO i/c walked into Harding's office with some typewritten pages in his hand.

'Morning, Harding – Chief Officer.' He sat down and tapped the sheets. 'What are we going to do about this fellow, Dettner?'

'Ah!' said Harding. 'Yes. I've got a copy of that report of Renfrew's.'

'According to Renfrew, by the time he got there with the tugs, the vessel was secured and fire hoses were in action. When she blew up, Renfrew, his tugmaster and helmsman were all knocked out and the tug was being dragged down by the sinking ship. This is as you saw it?'

'Yes, as I put in my report.'

'So Dettner not only got the harbour tug away safely but also the other tug with water cannon and picked up the men from the one that was sunk. To my mind, that calls for recognition – but what the hell's the good of a bloody gong to him?'

He cast an apologetic eye towards Jenna.

'If I might suggest – send copies of all reports, details of dead and injured to Admiralty and ask them to recognise appropriately.'

'Pass the buck, eh?'

'No,' said Harding, with a grin. 'Commended by the highest authority.'

Which was why, some days later, Admiral Everett called for Vice-Admiral Chalmers, gave him a wad of papers and told him to go away and study them at his leisure and for God's sake come up with an answer.

24

On Friday, Harding and Jenna attended the funerals at Ulsdorf. The two men who had been at the stern of the harbour tug had been buried at Fremenshaven but Renfrew's department had been represented there. The other three dockyard men were being buried at Fremenshaven on Friday afternoon where Harding and Jenna again attended. The dockyard was shut.

Jenna, watching Dettner both at Ulsdorf in the morning and at Fremenshaven in the afternoon, wondered if what he had said was true – that he wore his naval greatcoat, that it was a façade, it was the result of a rigorous training. She certainly could not fault his demeanour, the gentle kiss he gave to one elderly mother, the consoling clasp of one sobbing widow, the handshake with a teenager who was now the man of the house. Even the stoicism with which he bore a grasp on his arm where the vicious burn must have been more than painful. Controlled, she thought, totally in control.

She didn't hear Harding tell Dettner to come back to the naval base and returned to the WRNS officers' quarters to think over the day.

Harding had his own quarters at the Base. As a Captain he was not a Wardroom officer and only went there at the invitation of the Base Commander who was Mess President. But he had his sleeping cabin and his day cabin and it was here that he brought his guest. When his steward came, he sent for whisky.

'Captain Dettner will be dining with me,' he said.

Dettner did not object. He sank into one of Harding's club armchairs and accepted the glass of whisky thankfully. He was almost beyond speech and Harding let him be, watching him quietly behind the savouring of his own drink.

When he reckoned that the man had recovered sufficiently he said, 'It's been rather a morbid day. I thought this might be better than letting you go back to a deserted yard.'

The blue eyes contemplated him. The yard, of course, was not entirely deserted but would have the nightwatchmen there now. A gleam of amusement crept into them.

'Now, why,' wondered Dettner, 'should you think I'd go back to the yard?'

Harding bit back a snort of laughter.

'I'm sorry if I've interfered with a night of pleasure,' he said.

Dettner shook his head, smiling.

'I think a quiet drink, a good dinner, will suit me better than anything,' he said.

He was ready to talk, Harding recognised that. He recognised also that the man had little opportunity to talk with his peers. The nearest at the yard would be the ex-Paymaster who dealt with the accountancy side; but one didn't have a heart-to-heart with an employee as one might with an equal colleague or friend.

'I hoped it might,' Harding said. 'Though I fancy that if the yard rang through now with an emergency, you'd be off like a shot.'

Dettner shrugged, lurking amusement in his eyes. He's waiting to see what tack I'm going to take, Harding thought.

'You know the powers-that-be want to make some recognition to you for pulling the tugs out of the fire – and the people, of course,' he said. 'You saved a number of lives that day.'

'And lost how many – ten?'

'"Whoever saves one life saves the World entire",' murmured Harding.

'You're not Jewish.'

'No. How did you know that came from the Talmud?'

'Forbidden fruit.'

Harding sat back in his chair, exasperated.

'You're an educated, even erudite man,' he said. 'How the bloody hell did you put up with national socialism?'

'What do you think would have happened to my career if I had spoken against it?' Dettner asked, ready to try to explain. 'Remember, that in the beginning it brought employment, a renewal of pride. You agreed we should build more ships –

Lutzow, Scheer, Bismarck – Prinz Ludwig. But then there was the demand for *Lebensraum*, empire-building. Even so, we were welcomed in Austria, the Sudetenland, even Lithuania. By the time the real atrocities were coming to light, what could we do? Stauffenberg tried... Bonhoeffer... Even the German people suffered under the SS. I thank God I was at sea. But also there you dared not speak against Hitler. If you were reported, that was the end.'

'You must have known the war was lost when Italy kicked out Mussolini and changed sides. Couldn't you have kicked out Hitler, then?'

'We had no king as they had. Who would have prevailed against the Storm troopers? Would you have changed sides and fought with us against Russia?'

'Which is what Dönitz asked us to do when he took over.'

'Instead you let the Russians come through beyond Berlin. And now you suffer for that.'

Harding refreshed their drinks.

'Ye-es,' he said. 'We gave in to Eisenhower over that, I think. Did you follow the Nürnburg trials?'

Dettner shook his head.

'I was too busy being Master after God,' he said.

'I haven't heard that one.'

'Tugboat skipper.'

The steward came in to lay the table. Conversation over what was, in fact, an excellent dinner veered towards naval occasions and the Engineer Captain found him recounting tales he thought he had long forgotten of days in foreign ports, of reviews, of ceremonies, of pageantry.

'Good God,' he said, when the steward put port and marsala on the table. 'I must sound like the *Boys' Own Paper*!'

Dettner was laughing.

'If your people wish to reward me,' he said, 'give me a commission in the Royal Navy and a posting to Ceylon.'

'I wish we could,' said Harding. 'But – seriously?'

'Give me some sailing concessions. North Sea tramping is no good.'

They returned to the armchairs for their coffee. Harding, finding his guest totally relaxed, was satisfied. They talked a bit about the yard and its future and about *Neumark*. Captain Lausen had, fortunately, pulled himself together and found himself a Chief Officer and Chief Engineer. The mere fact of being able to offer employment to ex-colleagues helped to restore pride in himself. A first and second officer together with the two U-boat apprentices should be sufficient while voyages were restricted. A second engineer and crew members should not be difficult to find. The old U.O. wharf and its sheds were ready to receive cargo and the first sailing was scheduled for early in the next month.

'I must go,' said Dettner, standing up. 'I have greatly enjoyed this evening. Thank you.'

'So have I,' said Harding and escorted him down to his car.

The last shreds of daylight were fading from the summer sky. The night air was soft and warm. They paused to savour it, sailors both, assessing the weather it heralded. It augured well.

'Refreshed and ready to face all comers?' said Harding.

'Good God, no.' Dettner smothered a prodigious yawn. 'I would not have the strength to resist a Wren tonight.'

He got into the car, waved a cheerful hand and drove away. Harding, raising his eyebrows, felt a silent laugh tugging at his guts.

The yard was not reopening until Monday morning. Dettner, viewing the promised weather over breakfast on Saturday morning, told Mirsch to pack him an overnight bag and gave himself a couple of days off.

Harding came into the dockyard office early Monday morning. He found Dettner reading the divers' report on the damage to the dock wall caused by the explosion. It was, fortunately, not so severe as might have been feared.

'Jenna will be along in a little while,' said Harding. 'She's gone to check the arrival of the relief crews now you have made good the damage to the stern of the harbour tug. Incidentally, they have recovered the three bodies from the sunk tug and we'll be getting down to shifting the wreckage today.'

'Good. Now tell me, how may I repay your very kind hospitality of Friday night?'

Harding grinned.

'As a very junior officer, I remember going to a Marseilles harbour cafe where they had Apache dancing. As a senior officer I don't get the chance to do that sort of thing. I'd quite like to see some – low life.'

'You are not looking for *scènes vécues*!' said Dettner in mock horror, his eyes alight with laughter.

'No!' said Harding, scandalised. 'No, I am not looking for *scènes vécues*!'

'And what are they when they're at home?' asked Jenna at the door.

Dettner got to his feet, throwing an amused look at Harding who said, shortly, 'What they call "feelthy pictures" in Cairo.'

Jenna looked from one to the other, startled, but did not comment. A new light on both of them.

They went that night to Bremen.

'I would have preferred Hamburg,' said Dettner, 'but my petrol would not stretch.'

'And where do you get enough petrol even for Bremen?'

'That you do not ask.'

Harding did not get his fondly remembered Apache dancing but they found Sally Bowles and *Blue Angel* lookalikes in fishnet and made a brief visit to a bar filled with glamorously made-up visions in shiny, slinky frocks, where Harding was propositioned by one of the beautiful young men and Dettner watched him struggle, then took pity on him and whisked him off to a discreet cafe which accepted them despite their casual garb and served them an excellent dinner with good wine. It was well into the early hours of Tuesday morning by then and Harding was beginning to droop.

'That was an eye-opener,' he said as they drove back to the Base. 'I asked for it and – yes – I've enjoyed it! Thank you. But how do they all do it? – Black market, of course.'

25

In September the projected parliament Council at Bonn under the chairmanship of Konrad Adenauer came into being. Also, in early September *Neumark* tied up at the renovated U.O. wharf in the Port of London and Captain Lausen made a visit to Admiralty carrying a long box. He was greeted with some suspicion but insisted that his box must be given into the hands of Captain Sillifant. So Peter was sent for.

Chalmers, strolling into Peter's office from his own, next door, found him at his desk in rapt contemplation of a beautiful scale model of HMS *Moorhampton*, sitting in a sea of green, white-capped waves with a splendid froth at her bows.

'Good God!' he said. 'Where did that come from?'

'Dettner sent it for John,' said Peter. 'I don't know that I shall be able to give it up, though.' Very carefully he lifted it from its base to show that it was complete down to the keel with rudder and four propellers. 'Even the engine-room and cabins and mess decks,' he said, awe-struck, replacing it in the deep groove and lifting off the deck and superstructure.

Like a couple of schoolboys they explored its secrets.

'Complete in every detail – bar a crew,' said Chalmers. 'Has Dettner anything to say?' Peter looked at the accompanying note.

'Only an apology that it took so long to make – but they wanted it to be correct. And a hope that John will like it. I've half a mind to keep it here.'

He did not, however, and John's ecstatic letter of thanks reached Dettner some days later. It also detailed the first days at the new school where he was a boarder and bemoaned the necessity to leave his model at home. Just over a year, now, thought

Dettner, since he and Peter had puffed their unfit way to the top of Grey Tor; then to London and his swift transition to Fremenshaven and the Engineer Captain's office. Now, the yard was thriving and *Neumark* on her way to Hull, from there to the Hook and up north again to Esbjerg. Tramping.

The office door flung open and he looked up from his desk, from John's letter and the thoughts it had evoked, to see a burly figure in a shabby reefer and badgeless seaman's cap, advancing.

'Stolz!' he said in surprise.

The man was mouthing obscenities.

'I was your father's senior bloody Master,' he rasped. 'Why have you taken on that drunken shit, Lausen? Get out from that desk you pathetic little fucker.'

Dettner came round the desk. He was aware that Harding was in the doorway, blocking the scene from Jenna on the steps and that Mirsch had come to the passage door. He ducked under Stolz's swinging blow, kneed him in the stomach and slammed a fist in his face as he doubled over. The man crashed to the floor.

Jenna remembered Harding saying 'Paradoxical, like when you knock a man down and stand by to pick him up.'

She saw the big man struggling to sit up, saw Dettner bend and pull him up and thrust him into an armchair.

'All under control?' said Harding. 'We'll see you later.'

He pulled the door shut behind them and followed Jenna down the steps.

'That was smartly done,' she said.

'Oh, yes, he's no slouch,' said Harding. 'And, of course, he's learned it the hard way.'

Dettner was alone when they went back half an hour later. Two fingers on his left hand were bandaged together, the one acting as a splint for the other.

'Broke it on him, did you?' said Harding.

'Yes. I'm sorry about that. He was one of my father's skippers. He's been doing odd jobs at the Hamburg docks for three years. It – gets frustrating.' He frowned over the situation for a moment, then looked up with a smile. 'I shall have to get another ship. I have promised him the next one. Now – did you see what you came for?'

They had come to see the final raising and removal of the sunken ship and the start of repairs to the dockside wall which they discussed for a while together with the insurance claims.

Jenna was rather silent on the drive back to the Base. She was enjoying this posting and she knew that a good deal of that enjoyment came from the association with the man who was making such a success of a job he had never wanted. In a year's time the Allied Military Government would be replaced by the Allied High Commission, the Fremenshaven docks would be handed back to the Docks and Harbour Board and the Navy would withdraw. Already it was winding down: young Blair had gone some months ago; there was not much future for her. She could get another stripe which would probably mean an administrative position, not a 'hands-on' posting. As yet, there was no sign of any WRNS officer being posted to sea as a Chief Engineer. Russian merchant vessels, of course, had them but not, so far as she knew, such German merchantmen as were operating – certainly not English.

'What's on your mind, Jenna?' said Harding.

'Career prospects, sir,' she sighed.

Harding threw a quizzical glance at her.

'Do you reckon you'll need a career?' he asked.

'*Kinder, Kirche und Küche*?' she said. 'Not my style.' And yet—? 'I shall probably retire from the WRNS when we finish here.'

'And I shall probably be axed,' said Harding, grimly. 'There won't be many jobs going unless they need instructors – and you're more up to date than I am.'

They contemplated the peacetime future sadly.

Jenna went out to Ulsdorf again in the middle of October. The wall had presented some difficulties as repair had to be carried out by divers but it was now reported complete and, though she did not intend to inspect it personally, she wanted to be present at the final inspection. However, she found a slight hiatus. All the workforce were in one of the big sheds – it was time for their *mittagessen* though they often took that in shifts and certainly not all gathered together. She heard some triumphant singing and walked in, wondering. Even the naval diving team was there and she cornered their P.O.

'Sorry, Ma'am,' he said, grinning. 'They asked us to come in for a beer. It's the first anniversary of the reopening of the yard. Is it OK?'

'Yes, of course it is,' she said. 'Is the Director here?'

'Yes – he's over there, Ma'am, leading the singing.'

Jenna nodded.

'Give me a beer, P.O.,' she said. 'I don't suppose they'll mind if I join in.'

Thereafter it was another six weeks before she saw Dettner again and then it was at the U.O. wharf at Fremenshaven where *Neumark* was discharging cargo. The mate of the hold was on deck and the tallyman on the dockside, two derricks working together, one guyed over the side, the other plumbing the hatch. Dettner was by the shed, wearing a thick bridge coat with a U.O. Line skipper's cap, talking to Captain Lausen. Jenna, wrapped in a naval duffel coat with the hood up over her tricorne, approached them. She pushed back the hood and saluted them and Dettner touched the peak of his cap in acknowledgment, smiling. Lausen also touched his cap briefly as he left them and Dettner drew Jenna into the shelter of the shed.

'It is a long time since I have seen you,' he said. 'May I take you out tonight?'

'I should like that,' she said. 'Formal or casual?'

'As you wish.'

'Casual, please. We can be formal later – if you will come to the Wrens' Christmas dance.'

'Why do you invite me to these things?' he said, laughing.

'They are all I can ask you to,' she said. 'You don't have to come.'

'You have asked me so I will come,' he said. 'Now, what are you here to inspect?'

Again she did not know or ask where they went that night. They dined and danced and supped in the early hours where a small orchestra played Viennese waltzes as background music. And she never felt the bitter December chill.

Then it remained just to look forward to the Christmas dance which was to be held in the big hall at the Base, there being little room in the Officers' Quarters. It was festively decorated, there was a bar and the Marines' Dance Band had been given permission to play for them.

Jenna, putting on her long taffeta frock with its little matching jacket, soberly consulted her feelings. The others had invited officers from the Base, some of them knew officers from visiting ships including one Dutch and one Norwegian, but she was the only one whose guest was a native. She had a sudden fear that she might be exposing him to embarrassment but when he arrived she realised that he was fully aware that he was putting his head in the lion's jaws, so to speak, and was prepared to cope. She also realised that he was the only one in civilian dinner jacket though all, of course, wore wing collars and bow ties. Her first shock came early. One of the Dutch officers near them spoke of visiting a cruiser – a splendid ship, he said, came as reparations and had been the *Prinz Ludwig*, now called *Den Helder*. Dettner turned round.

'Commander van Houben,' he said. 'You speak of my old ship.'

The Dutchman looked at him. A broad smile spread over his face and he put out his hand.

'Captain Hans Dettner,' he said. 'You old sod!' He looked quickly at Jenna and made a laughing apology. 'We have known each other – oh – twenty years. Yes, we are looking after your old ship, Hans. She – er –' he waggled his hand, 'vibrates a bit at speed but so beautiful.'

He then bowed and asked Jenna to dance. When he returned her, she found her guest comfortably chatting with Captain Bailey and wondered why she had ever had misgivings. He got up, excused himself from Bailey and quietly swept her into the next dance.

Her second qualm came after the buffet supper. The atmosphere was becoming a little over-relaxed, the band was into romantic mood. The Third Officer in charge of the WRNS Quarters in the house at Ulsdorf came up. She was not tight but was well-primed; she was not unsteady but just a shade over-exaggerated in her movements. The band were embarking on *Tales from the Vienna Woods* and she told Dettner she had always longed to waltz with someone who really knew the true Viennese way. He took in her condition and looked regretful.

'No one,' he said, firmly, 'who danced in the Viennese way would do so in a dinner jacket. It must be danced in tails or in full-dress uniform and,' he considered her frock which was a cocktail sheath, 'a very full dress.'

Jenna looked at the couples dancing and had to admit he was right. They looked very rigid without the flying tails and the swinging skirts.

'You got out of that well,' she said. 'I could just see her taking a tumble.'

She met the amused gaze of blue eyes and knew that he was aware of what she had visualised. He shook his head in gentle reproof.

'Perhaps I should go now,' he said. 'As the senior Wren officer here, do I thank you?'

'I suppose you do,' she said. 'You can hardly go all round the Mess Committee.'

She went to the door with him and gave him her hand which he bowed over very correctly. Then he was gone. She went back into the hall and wished the dance would finish for it no longer held any appeal for her.

26

The New Year brought many new developments including the formation of NATO in April and the approval by the Occupying Powers in May of a Federal German Constitution known as the Basic Law. On a more personal plane, Dettner acquired another ship. She was smaller but more modern than *Neumark* and was called *Altstadt*. He offered her to Stolz whom he knew as a good seaman and told him to assemble his own crew. He wondered if he had overreached himself and would go bankrupt and sat at his desk, gazing at the picture of *Prinz Ludwig* and finding he didn't much care. He had come back in 1945 and in 1947 with nothing and could start again – if he wanted to.

Jenna was equally despondent. She had been offered the chance of promotion, as a Superintendent WRNS (Admin.) or else retirement at the conclusion of her present posting in May and had chosen the latter which meant that she had two months to go.

But she had only herself to consider. Hans Dettner, shifting his gaze to the window, where a pale blue March sky studded with hurrying clouds showed, thought of the workforce, the ships' crews and his responsibility for them. But the yard was viable and saleable – he didn't have to go on carrying them. Did he? The memory of Hoche in the water and the day after when Mirsch and Weiss had kept him alive; the two widows and three children in Ulsdorf and the men, five bodies lying on the quayside – the hymn sung at each funeral:

> Father in thy Gracious keeping,
> Leave we now thy servants sleeping.

He was as much responsible for them as he had been for the 900-odd ship's company in *Prinz Ludwig* and must decide in favour of their safety and well-being.

On his desk lay a letter informing him that the Wrennery was to close next week and his house would be returned to him. Perhaps it was this that had stirred his restless thoughts. To take back the house, to restore his old home, would surely be an anchor, a commitment, a tie. His thoughts strayed to Peter and Greystone, the old Admiral and Kate and John. Further back to the sunlit days when the two destroyers had lain at the quayside at Seahaven and the brisk young officer he had been then. His immense pride in the command of the heavy cruiser and the crushing misery of the last voyage to her home port of Wilhelmshaven. Now, the Director of the Ulsdorf Repair Dockyard and of U.&O. Shipping Line (fleet two ships) and in command of about half the number of men as in *Prinz Ludwig*. He got up from his desk, pulled on his leather jacket and went to the door. There he buttoned his metaphorical naval greatcoat and went down the steps and across the sprawling yard.

At the Naval Base, Jenna was reporting to Captain Harding. He could recognise her feelings at the present time – a sensation of being cast off into space. She had been in the WRNS for close on seven years and, as he knew only too well, the Navy was father and mother but once you left home had little more to do with you. He feared his own fate on the conclusion of this posting and had hoped to have heard of some future lined up for him.

'They will be taking on staff for NATO,' he remarked. 'Do you want to go on working abroad or is it back to England?'

'I'm absolutely blank on the subject,' she said. 'British shipbuilding's in a hell of a state. There's the marine experimental place at Teddington but there'll be masses of engineers after jobs and a woman still comes a poor second.'

'HAPAG are taking on more ships.' He eyed her quizzically. 'I hear the U.O. Line has increased its fleet, too.'

Jenna chuckled.

'He'll go broke if he's not careful,' she said. 'How on earth can he afford to pay another ship's crew?'

'A very shrewd operator, our *Herr Direktor*,' said Harding.

'And I gather his ex-Paymaster is something of a financial wizard.'

'Just as well, I should say,' said Jenna, broodingly. 'What do you make of him? Dettner, I mean. He's devious, slippery as an eel, always in command and utterly charming. And I'm hooked.'

'Yes,' said Harding, rather unkindly. 'He's been dangling you on his line for some time, hasn't he? What are you going to do about it?'

'You tell me,' she said. 'What can I do about it?'

'I can't help you there. But I'll tell you one thing.' Harding paused, wondering how to put it. 'If I were in a nasty situation – I'd trust that man with my life.'

Jenna gazed at him for a moment.

'Well – you can't say better than that, can you?' she said at last.

'Tell you what,' he said. 'That British coaster's completion date is next week. Go out and see it with the Master.'

'That will insult his Excellency, won't it?' she said.

Harding laughed.

'He might be pleased to see you,' he said.

So Jenna drove herself out to Ulsdorf the following week and went aboard the coaster which had suffered a fire in a hold while unloading at Fremenshaven and been sent up-river to the repair yard. She found the British Master, a tall, spare Yorkshireman, on the deck of his vessel talking with Dettner, who introduced them.

'Captain Royden will be leaving on the tide,' he said. 'Unless you are not satisfied with the repairs.'

'I'd better see them,' she said, straight-faced and followed Royden down the hatchway. 'You're quite satisfied, Captain?'

'Aye – it's a good job and quicker than I'd feared. I'll be able to get back to Fremenshaven and start loading this afternoon.'

They found Dettner, awaiting them on deck, uncharacteristically idle. 'Passed,' said Jenna. 'Goodbye, Captain. Safe voyage.'

She and Dettner walked away from the jetty across the yard towards the office. She felt with a sharp pang how she would miss the now so familiar place, the busyness, the sights, the sounds, the coffee in the office.

But he walked her past the steps and out of the gate, across the lane and through the gate to the house. She saw it was curtainless and unoccupied.

'I miss them coming back at night,' he remarked, simply, as he unlocked the door.

Despite its uncompromising exterior, she recognized the fine proportions of the hall, the gracious solidity of the oak staircase rising and curving round to the first floor. She stopped in the middle of the bare floor and looked at him.

'Will you marry me?' he said.

'Why – do you want someone to look after the house?' her pisky said and instant amusement lit his eyes.

'No – I want a Chief Engineer.'

'That's good,' she said with a sigh of relief. 'I'm not very domesticated.'

He laughed.

'That does not matter. I shall convert the top floor to an apartment for Mirsch and his wife – she is a good cook.' Perceiving a possible error, he retrieved it, smoothly. 'The rest of the house I shall leave to you. If you will say yes?'

'Oh, yes,' she said. 'You know, you only once gave me any idea of how you felt – that Sunday – I came and you were going to church.' She looked around the bare hall with the cream walls and the pale blue woodwork. 'What a romantic place for a proposal!'

'I'm not romantic,' he assured her. 'But I have wanted you since you first came into my office with Blair.'

'Why did you wait so long?' she teased him.

'I could not ask you to share my quarters at the yard' he protested.

'What will you do with them?'

'Keep them – to escape to.'

They strolled through the house, perfectly attuned.

'You have a mistress, I suppose?' she remarked, as they went upstairs.

'Yes. She has no use for me at present. But if she calls, I shall go.'

'The sea,' murmured Jenna. 'I shan't stop you. Not romantic, my foot!'

He paused to kiss her and she clung tightly for a moment.

'Otherwise,' he said, 'what is past, is finished.'

She accepted that soberly. Obviously he had not been celibate. She would not have expected it.

'You do know what you are doing?' he said. 'Your country, your nationality – your family?'

'Yes,' she said. 'My family and I parted when my father died. My country – well, you're an anglophile, aren't you?'

'Very much so.'

In May, HMS *Blackavon* was decommissioned and the White Ensign lowered from the flagstaff for the last time. Naval and military personnel were dispersed in various directions and Fremenshaven shook itself to settle down again as an unoccupied commercial port. At the same time Hans Gerhardt Dettner and Jenna Anne Polruthan were quietly married at a civil ceremony there and returned to their newly refurbished and furnished home in Ulsdorf where they were welcomed by Otto and Gerda Mirsch and a guard of honour that stretched halfway to the port, of dockyard staff. The following day Pastor Müller was to conduct an equally quiet church service.

It was once again in early September that Peter Sillifant strolled into Chalmers's office.

'Guess who I've had a call from,' he said. 'Dettner. He rang from the docks.'

'What, here? London? What had he to say?'

' "May I pay you an informal visit?" ' quoted Peter, smiling. 'So I said "Delighted. Come aboard".'

'Sounds as if you've had this exchange before,' said Chalmers. 'Tell them to bring him up here.'

When he arrived Peter was almost transported back to Seahaven. The same spare figure, the same lean browned face and keen blue eyes. Older, of course, they were both 11 years older and with a wealth of experience in the intervening years. He gripped their hands and explained himself. He was relieving Lausen for one trip – just a short one to the Port of London and back.

'Brought the Chief Mate with you?' asked Chalmers, crudely.

Dettner paused.

'No.' He smiled, disarmingly. 'I have left her in charge of the yard. She did not feel like a sea trip just now.'

'Ah! Planning a big family?'

'No, no. Two will do – one for the yard and one for the navy. I hear it is possible we might be able to rebuild the Merchant Marine soon. Is it so?'

Chalmers rubbed his head.

'It's on the cards. Also that you can reestablish consular and commercial relations abroad.' He went on with slow deliberation. 'When an Ambassador is again appointed to the Court of St James, I am advocating that they send you as Senior Naval Attaché.'

Dettner stiffened, his eyes fixed on Chalmers's face.

'But we have no navy,' he said slowly.

'The Americans are putting out feelers about rearming you. I think it is possible in the next year or two.'

'You give me a lot to think about and to hope for. Incidentally, we were glad to hear that Captain Harding was posted to Plymouth. He was a little anxious about his future.' Dettner stood up. 'I must go back to *Neumark*. Thank you for seeing me. Could either or both of you dine with me tonight?'

Both gentlemen found they could and arranged a rendezvous. Then Peter escorted him down to the street.

When he got back to the office, Chalmers shook his head smiling.

'I told you – a bright spark. He'll be the Grand Admiral before he's finished.' He looked around the shabby, custard-painted office with satisfaction. 'Married an English girl, too.'

'I think she'd call herself a Cornishwoman,' murmured Peter.

Dettner, having paid off his taxi at the docks, paused to view his ship, as she lay, secured to the quayside. Black painted, with her buff superstructure and the black and buff stack, old Albrecht's colours, she had a certain workmanlike grace. She was not what he wanted, not what he had trained for, not what in *Prinz Ludwig* he had attained. But she was his, as the successful yard was his and his beloved Jenna and the coming child. And his two good English friends coming to dine with him tonight. He was content – midway between the heights and the deep.